SMOKO

F.E. BEYER

Sandfly Press, 2023

www.febeyer.com

Cover design: Mindbomb Design and Sosa.kl

Never forget that the human race with technology is just like an alcoholic with a barrel of wine.

Ted Kaczynski

The Unabomber Manifesto: Industrial Society and its Future

So when you felt the shadow of the rate-checker breathing down your neck you knew what to do if you had any brains at all: make every move more complicated, though not slow because that was cutting your own throat, and do everything deliberately yet with a crafty show of speed.

Alan Sillitoe

Saturday Night and Sunday Morning

Prologue

I felt anxious. Would they hold me partly to blame? I feared someone would say, 'He's your mate. You must have known about this.' But in the immediate aftermath of discovering the missing nuts and bolts nobody paid any attention to me. Mavis opened the bike storage and, coughing because of the dust in there, fussed about finding the right-sized bikes and helmets for everybody. While the others smoked or drank coffee, I hid by the lockers eating gingernuts. Then Joyce came by to tell me there was a meeting.

Tired Mavis with eyebags like deep purple bruises stood before us and said, 'The bicycles need maintenance. We don't want any more accidents, so we're cancelling delivery for today.' I wondered if this was the royal we or if she'd already got instructions from HQ. It must have been agony for her, calling them to say that things had gone badly wrong at her depot.

'We haven't had any bloody accidents,' Joyce said. 'We've had attempted murder—multiple counts of attempted murder.'

Mavis nodded in agreement but verbally kept things in check. 'Alright, don't dramatise the situation. I know you've had a fright but let me handle things. We'll start again tomorrow by delivering two days' mail in one. Today the mail load was light—so it'll be okay. You can all go home and relax now.'

'What about Dawn?' I asked. Mavis's eyes bored into me. A look of pure poison. A normal reaction from her so I tried not to read anything into this withering look.

'Nothing from her yet. I'll keep trying to get a hold of her. Now go on, piss off home, all of you.'

1

I sat on an uncomfortable chair with a thick manual in front of me. As I read about the history of the postal service, two more trainees, a woman and a man, arrived.

'Cutting it fine, guys,' Norm told the newcomers, tapping his watch. 'All right, eight-thirty, let's get started. Don't worry, I'm gonna keep things light but make sure you listen, eh! I learnt to spot daydreamers in the army. You don't want to head into combat with somebody thinking about how to cook a Thai green curry.'

Norm didn't bore us with endless details from the manual. However, he spent an inordinate amount of time on security stuff. He opened his eyes crazy wide when addressing us, making everything he said seem important.

'You should hide your uniform behind your towels on the washing line, so it doesn't get stolen. We don't want someone impersonating a postie terrorising the neighbourhood.'

Was he serious? I couldn't tell. What did my fellow inductees think? The woman chewed her pen and rubbed a red spot on her cheek. The man repeatedly passed his hand over his head, as though looking for hair he'd lost years ago. Their expressions gave nothing away.

Norm warned us to be honest about recording the number of letters we sorted. 'If the team leader doesn't get you for writing up too many letters, the algorithms will.'

We got paid for the number of letters sorted rather than hours worked. What if I was slow?

After a couple of hours in the training room, Norm gave the okay for us, his three newbies, to stand up and stretch. He then took us for a look around the aeroplane-hangar-like depot.

'Look at these sorting machines.' Norm pointed at a gaggle of contraptions that looked like giant printers from the 1980s topped with black induction pipes. 'Nine years ago they cost eighty million. Now they're done, obsolete. Can only read envelopes with barcodes, not actual addresses. No good.'

Eighty million for the machines in Wellington or the entire country? How could a barcode give an address?

Before I could ask, a guy with a ginger beard and hands black with grease jumped out from behind a partly disassembled mammoth and said: 'They wanted these bloody things scrapped, but now they've changed their minds. Can't afford new ones, so I'm putting them back together again.'

'Typical, eh,' Norm replied.

The man with greasy hands looked satisfied with this comment and got back to work. He started tapping the side of a machine with a spanner, which caused an arrhythmic beat to echo around the depot.

For me, this inefficiency of taking things apart and putting them together again was good news. I'd feared the post office would be a super-organised place to work. I conquered the urge to ask about the eighty million dollars and the barcodes. Life had taught me not to show too much curiosity too soon.

The other two trainees lived less than ten kilometres from the central depot and so didn't get lunch money. Norm and I did. We had an allowance of thirty dollars each on his company credit card. Norm chose a flash gastropub for lunch. He was flirty with the waitress. It surprised me she didn't seem to mind. She couldn't have been much more than twenty.

Norm had asked how old we thought he was in the training room. Before anybody could answer, he said, 'Forty-six. Don't look it though, eh?'

We all nodded. He did look good for his age.

After the waitress had smilingly taken our orders, Norm's mouth turned my way. To stop him from talking shop, I asked about his military days.

'You'll never get to that level physically, never experience those extremes,' he said referring to his training to get into the Special Forces. 'After fourteen days, I was ripped as, mate. But on the last exercise, jumping off the top of a four-metre wall, I broke my ankle. I got invited to do the training again when I healed, but decided I'd wanted to join the Special Forces for the wrong reasons.'

After the army, he worked as security for weapons inspectors in Saddam's Iraq. 'I reported to Chief Weapons Inspector Hans Blix, who in turn reported to Kofi Annan. I was only a couple of steps from George Bush. If I said,

"Let's get out of here" when inspecting a facility, we got the fuck out!'

Eyeballs popping out of his skull, Norm used what was available on the table to reinforce my understanding of the chain of command. The Secretary-General of the United Nations Annan was the saltshaker, Blix the pepper, and Norm himself the large tomato sauce bottle. As he arranged these objects, I noticed the vascularity of his forearms. The bastard was in great shape.

The waitress, still smiling, brought Norm his Thai green mussels with ciabatta bread. His comment regarding daydreaming about Thai green curry during the morning session indicated a delicious lunch had been on his mind. He looked disapprovingly at my choice of Caesar salad.

The training session proved to be an easy half-day of theory. Driving home, my stomach and mood felt light. I congratulated myself for having a salad for lunch, and for making progress towards my first postie payday.

To celebrate, I took a walk in the park over the road from my flat. I admired the skeletal oak trees standing out against the green bush, bent down to smell the wet grass, and smiled at a family walking their dog. Things I'd never normally do. This euphoric outing was cut short as wind-driven horizontal rain arrived.

In my room, I quickly dozed off with Brian Eno's *Music for Airports* in my ears. I occupied the flat's only bedroom. For her own makeshift sleeping space, my flatmate Rachel, had curtained off half the lounge. My room was big and the rent cheap: maybe forty dollars less than what you'd expect to pay a week. It'd been the second place I visited on my flat hunt. The guy moving out told me Rachel, the leaseholder, camped in her van half the time. I texted this Rachel. She said the other guy approved of me, so I could move in. I knew it wouldn't be the perfect place to live but I was too lazy to look for anywhere else. In terms of setting my room up, I had bought a bed but no other furniture.

After a forty-five-minute nap, I woke up refreshed and ready for an evening of YouTube videos. I would need a coffee and a tuna sandwich with canned corn and peas on the side—one of my go-to meals when in saving mode. Rachel arrived home as I waited for the kettle to boil. In her fifties, she limped because of hip and ankle issues.

'Hi, what time did you knock off? You were working today, right?' She asked.

'Yeah, I was. Pretty early today.'

Small talk and coffee made, I hurried to my bedroom, plate in one hand, mug in the other. To eat, I sat on the side of the bed with the plate in my lap.

Before touching my computer, I fastidiously wiped any residual tuna oil off my fingers with a paper towel. Satisfied my hands were clean, I opened my browser and found a documentary on YouTube about Hermann Göring that looked good. Nothing like watching a docu about the Nazi leadership if you want to relax. But then the bedroom door opened, and Rachel shuffled in weighed down by a bulky dehumidifier clutched to her stomach. She put the machine down and fumbled with the plug.

'Rachel, what are you doing?'

She turned her head and regarded me with surprise. Her jaw dropped making her look like a gaping sideshow clown. If I'd had a ping pong ball to throw, I would have aimed for her mouth. Composing herself, Rachel gave me a sheepish grin.

'Ed! I forgot you were here.'

What? Was she senile at such a tender age? We'd spoken in the kitchen fifteen minutes ago.

'I've got to put the dehumidifier on—it's part of the rental agreement. We've had black mould here before. Sorry I didn't knock. I'll let you get back to whatever you were doing.' She turned on the machine and closed the door behind her. Rachel's having come into my room unannounced worried me.

That night I dreamt of Norm and Hans Blix visiting a suspected weapons-making facility in Baghdad.

'Look what we have here, Hans, bloody black mould-making machines.' Norm said.

'Ja. Saddam is inventive with biological weapons,' Hans replied, patting the side of one of the machines that looked suspiciously like mail sorters. 'Black mould spores are like mustard gas for people's lungs.' Hans's German accent was stronger in my dream than when I'd seen him on the news. And, unfairly, he'd adopted a Göring-like slicked back hairstyle.

'I've got this. Nothing some plastic explosive can't handle,' Norm began what looked like big pieces of chewing gum on each machine.

Instead of an explosion, my alarm went off—ten to six, time to get up. I ventured into the kitchen to prepare my bowl of Weet-Bix and a cup of instant coffee. The kitchen and lounge were open plan, so I could hear Rachel snoring gently behind her curtain. After wolfing down my breakfast, I washed my bowl and spoon and ignored her dirty plates that had been in the sink for several days.

2

The boxy building I parked in front of rather ruined the aesthetics of a suburban street lined by attractive houses. Inside, black plastic sorting cases lined up in uneven rows on a beige linoleum floor. Before seven in the morning, a trolley stood in front of each case stacked with grey plastic trays full of letters. The place smelled strongly of wet paper and disinfectant, with subtle hints of metal and glue in the background. A lot of my immediate future would be spent in this space. Over the next week, the postie crew at the depot taught me how to sort letters and handle the delivery vehicle After that, the team leader gave me two suburban mail runs to look after.

I kept a low profile at the depot. At thirty-two, I felt like a shy teenager around the grim-faced, fast-moving team of posties. But if I stayed silent too long, I worried they'd peg me as a weirdo.

On my tenth day, I decided to try and get into a conversation. I sat at one of the particle board tables in the smoko room looking through yesterday's paper and dunking gingernuts in my instant coffee. Two of my fellow posties, Dawn, with hair dyed bright red, and the strongly built Ross, sat at an adjacent table barking at each other about the daily dockets. 'Doesn't make any difference how you fill it out, Dawn. Inside the depot, they pay you for the letters you sort, and outside for the time it takes you to deliver. They assume you take two fifteen-minute breaks.'

'What you don't know, smart arse, is that I put in lost time for things like processing mis-sorts and impromptu meetings—it doesn't affect my pay, but it does affect my performance times.'

'This isn't the bloody Olympics.'

'You might think I'm a middle-aged idiot, Ross, but unlike you, I've been here more than five minutes and know what I'm talking about.'

Ross rolled his eyes but didn't respond and Dawn turned her attention to peeling a mandarin. This was my opportunity to speak, although I had nothing to add about the dockets. I put down my coffee and tried to think of something positive to say about the job. But coming out with an opener like 'The job is great, we are so lucky, right?' would've been out of character. Too enthusiastic. I went with, 'The good thing about this job is that you never touch a computer.'

They both looked at me. Was I talking to them? My comment had come out of the blue. Awkward. I feared they'd ignore me. But no, this wasn't a cliquey workplace.

'Is that what you used to be, a computer guy?' Ross asked. He held his hands out and typed on a ghost keyboard. I had to be careful, I didn't want to get painted with that brush. A computer geek I was not.

'No, no, I'm not a big fan of working on computers, especially if it means doing spreadsheets and things like that. A couple of the managers I've had in the past loved Excel. They constantly created coloured spreadsheets that we had to fill out.' Nervous, I had started to ramble.

Ross looked confused. Hadn't he heard of Excel? He can't have been much more than thirty. Lucky him if he hadn't. Or was he having me on?

I helped him out. 'Excel is a program used for doubling up admin records, financial calculations, and a bunch of other stuff.'

'I see.' Ross continued to look confused.

'I like Excel, it's logical,' said Dawn, using the back of her hand to wipe mandarin juice off her chin.

'Yes, the problem with me is I'm not detail-oriented, so Excel doesn't appeal.' I reckoned that was diplomatic, rather than telling Dawn to fuck off because Excel was an awful Satanic invention.

'I've noticed you aren't a detail guy,' said Ross.

'How'd he get this job then?' Asked Dawn, her tone all accusation.

'Some people are good at interviews,' said Ross.

It surprised and pleased me that Ross had noticed something about my personality. And then I thought, shit being a postie was about being meticulous when it came to redirections, holds, PO boxes, etc., and now these guys thought I didn't give a fuck about such details. So much for a successful foray into the realms of small talk.

'I'm off to deliver,' I said. I rinsed my plastic cup in the sink and grabbed my yellow and red raincoat off the back of the chair I'd been sitting on.

'That's a short break,' Dawn said, 'you've been in this room less than ten minutes.'

'It'll take me a long time to deliver the mail. I'm still getting used to the job.'

'You'd bloody better get on with it then.' Dawn said.

'Give the kid a break, Dawn,' Ross said. He rolled his eyes again, I guessed to indicate what a pain in the arse Dawn was.

Cutting my break short proved to be a good move because delivery took me six hours. I returned to a deathly quiet depot. Everybody else had delivered their mail and headed home hours ago. To my relief, the team leader's office door was closed and the light off. I'd already figured out she wasn't the friendliest. Instead of feeling lonely and slow, I felt a sense of achievement from at having completed the day's work. It'd been a heavy day in terms of the volume of letters. When I'd seen the trays of letters loaded on my trolley in the morning, I considered quitting there and then.

As the last to leave, I had to set the alarm. For a moment I couldn't remember the code. Was it 1018? Yes ... but what if I put in the wrong number? Should I call somebody to double-check the code? No, whoever I called would be pissed off at being bothered after hours. Tentatively I entered 1018 into the keypad and hit the button to activate the alarm. A warning beep sounded. I got the hell out of there. I waited nervously in my car praying that the alarm didn't go off. It didn't. At last, I could head home.

3

The next morning, I got to work early enough to grab a coffee in the smoko room before sorting. Unlike the sorting floor, the smoko room had a window. However, darkness still covered the fascinating vista of the car park at this time of the morning. So, I checked out the walls covered with posters and newspaper clippings.

'Salsa classes on Tuesday nights.'

No, thank you.

'Postie Retires After 42 Years.'

Bog help us.

Then, what luck! I found today's paper on one of the tables. The local suburban paper mind, not a serious newspaper like *The Dominion Post*. The front page featured a story about rats. The local exterminator was getting lots of callouts. In the cold weather, the rodents sought shelter inside people's houses. A real nuisance, the rats left droppings. If they couldn't find food, the rats chewed on everything: the pipes, the walls, the furniture. You could tell the size of a specimen from the teeth marks. 'The largest one

I've trapped this year was the size of my Chihuahua,' read a quote from the exterminator. That didn't sound very big.

Ross stormed into the smoko room, struggled out of a faded yellow and red raincoat, and set about making an instant coffee. He sat down at another table and took rapid sips from his plastic cup. His hair stuck up around the crown of his head, giving him the air of a schoolboy badly rested after playing video games late into the night. I recognised the 'God, another day' expression on his face. I took advantage of having something to talk about.

'You seen this article about rats, Ross?'

'No?' He looked at me in wonder, as If I'd materialised out of thin air. 'Let's have a look.'

I got up and handed him the paper.

'Hey, this is today's paper! Awesome.'

I gave him a few minutes to read it and then said, 'Something fishy about the story. What kind of rat exterminator would have a Chihuahua? I don't buy it. These journalists will do anything to flesh out a story. What do you reckon?'

'You might have something there. I bloody admire rats, resourceful animals. Did you know they can't vomit? For every new food source one rat acts the taster, either managing to stomach it or dying for the greater good.'

'Wow, interesting.' He'd given me a far better response than I'd expected. Maybe, it'd be worth getting to know this Ross.

Further chatting with Ross would have to wait because it was time for the morning briefing. Team Leader Mavis stood in front of the workers on the sorting room floor. A well-built woman in her fifties with spiky black hair, tattooed forearms, and a gravelly voice, today she had smoke coming out of her ears.

'If anybody else rolls their Kurrus, the pilot program is off. A failure. We'll be off our electric Swiss three-wheelers and back on push bikes. One person has rolled a Kurrus so far and by dumb luck didn't get injured. But others have tipped over their trailers. It's got to stop.'

I looked around at the other posties. Hardly a crew of Hell's Angels who'd been driving their delivery vehicles recklessly. Quite the opposite, their faces looked cautious and conscientious.

'If all eyes at HQ weren't on us before, believe me, they are now,' Mavis continued. 'Come on guys, we've worked too bloody hard for this to be taken away from us. We need to show them we can do it. It's an honour to be chosen as the pilot depot for the Kurrus. No more slogging it out on push bikes, don't you guys love it?'

The team assumed the question to be rhetorical.

The Kurrus had been introduced for mail delivery in Switzerland five years earlier. Now New Zealand wanted to catch up with those slick Europeans. A three-wheeler powered by an electric battery, the Kurrus—singular Kurrus, plural also Kurrus—was a PR coup for Post HQ. They could brag about how environmentally friendly the new vehicles were.

I found this laughable. How could they be more environmentally friendly than push bikes?

At the front of the Kurrus was a box-shaped container with handlebars behind it. The back of the vehicle featured a double-doored 'cupboard' with shelves. If you had more mail than would fit in the front box, side panniers, and cupboard, you could attach a trailer. With the trailer, you had to take corners slowly. So many posties tried to overpack the back cupboard to avoid taking a trailer.

'It's not all doom and gloom,' Mavis continued, 'today is the morning tea shout.'

'Woohoo ... sausage rolls again!'

Mavis frowned. 'I hope you're not taking the piss with that comment, Ross. Get back to your sorting and we'll see you in the smoko room for morning tea at ten.'

Three hours later, we headed to the smoko room where cheesecake, sausage rolls, and lollies awaited. No company-provided morning tea in New Zealand can be called complete without sausage rolls. Everybody had a cup of tea or coffee in hand. The topic around the crumb-covered tables was the Kurrus vehicles, which, so far, I'd found fairly easy to handle. While munching on a sausage roll, I now had the chance to listen to the other posties make comments about them.

'First time I saw all you guys head out on those econumbers I was choked up. Beautiful, what we've done here.'

'Makes you think! Plug the fucking things in and they go all day. Fourteen dollars a week it costs to charge them.'

'But twenty thousand to buy one and they don't even keep you dry. I still want an electric push bike.'

'Yeah, bring back the bikes.'

'Dream on!'

After predictions on the amount of mail that would arrive Saturday, an old-timer named Joyce whose scrunched paper skin was the work of a million cigarettes and UV rays, steered the conversation towards another favourite topic: retirement.

'How much you reckon you need to be comfortable?' Before anyone else could, she answered her own question, 'Two hundred thou minimum in the bank plus having the mortgage on the house paid off.' Going by her skin, I'd have guessed Joyce to be over ninety. However, her thighs, built by decades of delivering mail on a bicycle, would've put prime Arnold Schwarzenegger to shame. In truth, she wasn't much past sixty.

'Our plan is to sell the house and live in a campervan, travel around, go kayaking and mountain biking,' said Dawn.

'What about winter, be brutal in a caravan, won't it?' I asked.

'My husband already insulated it.'

'He still alive then, Dawn. Thought you would've killed him by now,' Joyce said.

Having seen Dawn have a go at Ross the other day about the dockets, I expected her to explode. However, she gave Joyce a nasty look, nothing more. As she was the team's most senior member, I guess it didn't pay to mess with Joyce. Even so, Dawn's reaction struck me as odd.

After morning tea, I went to get a coat from my locker. Ross approached me there and said, 'Twenty thousand each, those Kurrus. Ten of those fucking machines worth the rest of your life. I don't own a house and I'm not practical enough to insulate a caravan. I'll need a lot more than two hundred thousand for retirement! I'd like to smash those Swiss contraptions with a sledgehammer the day I leave this job.'

Ross's face spasmed. Breathing deeply, he managed to collect himself and move on. 'By the way, you plan to go home on your second break?'

'Yeah, how'd you know? I did so yesterday. Mavis has put me on run six. It's near my flat.'

'Careful, Mavis can see where your machine is at all times. They've got GPS on them. Don't go over your fifteen-minute break time. She'll see that your Kurrus has been stationary for too long.'

'But I don't think she'd look at the data that closely. I'm sure she has better things to do than calculating who's taking an eighteen-minute break.'

'She'll look, mate. With her it's a case of the information being in the wrong hands. She likes to have control—to have one over you for that crucial moment. She's an example of a small person using her tiny amount of power to the max.'

'Thanks for the advice, Ross, always good to have info on the boss.'

Because of the sausage rolls inside me, I found sitting on the Kurrus difficult for the first hour of delivery. My digestive system had dealt with the problem by the time I reached the Masonic Retirement Village. 'Hope it's not all bills today, mate,' one white-haired gent said. 'Haven't heard that before, mate,' I wanted to say to him. He wasn't the only one waiting by the mailbox. 'No good, it's no good,' grumbled a hair-in-rollers octogenarian. 'The mail was slow before, but now it only comes every two days, it's even worse. When I get my *TV Guide* the week is nearly over.' I felt bad for her, and I couldn't tell her to check online. Reliant on the mail and TV, here lived relics of an ancient civilisation.

The Tainui Retirement Village had a great view of the mountains, but the residents were less active than at the Masonic. One old guy with a bandage on his head staggered out his front door and thanked me profusely for the Pizza Hut flyer I handed him. I hoped for some old know-it-all to materialise and lecture me about the mountains. 'Stratus clouds hanging off their leeward side now, see there! The mountains rose above a group of cumulus clouds early this morning. Lenticular clouds covered them not long after you dropped off the wrong mail the other day, young man ...' But no such fucking luck.

Five hundred odd mailboxes into my run, not that I counted, the clouds thickened and the mountains disappeared. I turned onto a street with rusty, sharp-edged mailboxes stuffed with old slug-eaten newspapers. My soft hands got bloody trying to get letters in. Bleeding on a letter? Residents would complain. I coloured over the blood stains on a couple of envelopes with a black marker pen. Not in the training manual Norm had given us, but this trick worked. I needed a break but decided it'd be best not to go home. To drive there, eat something, and then drive back to the next delivery point would take more than fifteen minutes. So, I got a filled roll at the Cambodian Bakery and headed over to the church cemetery. I beeped the electric motor of my Kurrus off, dismounted, and walked around reading the headstones while munching my roll:

Here rest the earthly remains of Henry George,
Who was born June 17, 1842,

And killed in action Nov 6th, 1860.
The trumpet shall sound and the
Dead shall be raised incorruptible.

Back on the job, I spotted a postie from our rival company, DY Mail. Anonymous because his visor was pulled down, he rode his motorbike across immaculately manicured grass berms, leaving tyre tracks without a care in the world. I burned with envy. With all our rules and regulations, we would never compete with those guys.

'Hey, is that solar-powered, buddy?'

Someone was shouting at me. Where were they? Across the road, I spotted a small man with a scraggy beard wearing a tea-cosy hat. Even from five metres away, I caught a whiff of his BO. He looked like a rough sleeper.

'No mate, it isn't.'

'Well then, you should put some solar panels on it.'

I couldn't decide if he was joking.

'Yeah, it might make it go faster,' I shouted back, trying—without slowing down—to replicate his friendly enthusiasm. But talking and driving the Kurrus at the same time didn't work out and I clipped a power pole. One of my back wheels lifted off the ground, the Kurrus hesitated to decide whether it wanted to tip over or not and then thankfully came back down on all three wheels. The trailer, however, crashed onto its side with a clang. I got off the trike and righted the trailer but the red paint on the side panel was scraped and the mudguard dented. At the least, this would be two forms to fill out and a telling-off. At worst? Could the pilot program be called off? Would I become a pariah? 'If it wasn't for that idiot, we'd still be going up hills on our electric numbers'—or was a reversion to push bikes what everybody wanted? I told myself to calm down, the big deal was rolling the vehicles, not tipping trailers.

Tea-cosy Head had followed me. He was laughing his arse off.

'Where'd you learn to drive, Tictac? How long you been a postie?'

'Jesus Christ himself couldn't drive,' I answered. A stupid thing to say, but unexpected and it left the guy flummoxed. He scratched a hairy cheek, trying to think of a response. Before he opened his mouth, I drove off to my next delivery point, some hundred metres down the road.

When I got back to the depot, Dawn was still unloading her trike. Her eyes went straight to the damage on my trailer. 'Well,' she said dryly, 'I guess that's the equivalent of falling off your bike. We used to say you weren't a postie until you'd taken a tumble.'

I suspected Dawn would make sure everybody got to know I'd had this little accident. But this was it, at last, I felt like one of the team.

4

Finding the right slots for the letters on the sorting case was taking me ages. I went to the toilet, got some gingernut biscuits out of my locker, made a coffee, and drank it at my case—this was not allowed, but nobody noticed. None of these measures cleared my head. I'd never get the mail sorted. I started to look around for a distraction, for something to entertain me for a moment, so getting back to sorting would be easier. Everybody else was getting on with the job. Some tapped letters along the rows until they found the right spot, others had better hand-eye coordination and hit the target first up. Half the team pushed hard, the rest had more of a tortoise than hare philosophy.

Finally, something came along to break the boredom. Looking over the top of my sorting case, I noticed a partly eaten sandwich sitting in Dawn's cubbyhole for missorted letters. As a sign of my increased confidence around the depot, I yelled out to her:

'Hey Dawn, what's with the sandwich? Don't leave your half-finished food out. Put it in the fridge or your locker.'

Because of her short stature, I couldn't see Dawn over her sorting case, I just heard her disembodied croak, 'Yeah, I saw it already. It's not mine, I don't want to touch it. Why would I put a sandwich in my cubbyhole? Tell Mavis about it.'

'Why don't you want to touch it? It's in plastic.'

Mavis, her hearing supersonic, came out of her office. She was not impressed.

'Food isn't allowed on the sorting floor! I don't care if it's in plastic. Whoever put that there had better bloody throw it away.'

No one owned up. For the next couple of days, the sandwich stayed. Dawn worked around it.

'The bastard who put it there will eventually grow a conscience,' Dawn said, showing admirable patience.

That Saturday out on my run, I found the plastic-protected sandwich in the side compartment of my Kurrus. A close look revealed chicken and cranberry inside wholemeal bread. I suspected Johnno the Brummie to be the culprit. Ross had told me to look out for Johnno, an old salt known as a practical joker.

I was dead tired when I got back to the depot because of the huge load of mail I'd delivered, so I forgot to throw the sandwich out. Monday, my Kurrus didn't smell as bad as I'd feared. I decided to put the sandwich in Johnno's vehicle. 'And what do you think you're doing, son?' He had caught me in the act. I threw the sandwich at him without a great deal of force and missed. Laughing, he picked it up and put it in Dawn's Kurrus. And so, it began.

That sandwich kept doing the rounds between the three of us, turning up in rain jacket pockets and mail panniers. It was good fun hiding the sandwich, balm for mail sorting blues. However, one day in a fit of anger I threw it out. An act of desperate nihilism to be sure. I'd found it in my front pannier while loading up, its plastic container now held together by a couple of rubber bands.

'Oh, what's wrong with you?' Dawn asked, she'd seen me do it. I'd been caught not just throwing but slamming the sandwich into the bin. I must have looked a right nutter from Dawn's point of view. 'Not playing our little game anymore? You about to go postal on us? I'm always waiting for someone to freak out and run amok. Thought it'd be Mavis until your weird mate Ross came along. I've always thought Johnno was a candidate too. Wouldn't have picked you though. You're a lovely young man, Ed. So, let's have it. What's the problem?'

'It's these referendum voting papers—they'll take ages to deliver.'

'Stop feeling sorry for yourself boy,' Dawn snapped, 'you've got to keep going. Have a cup of coffee, a biscuit—something to perk you up.'

Some cocaine would've been good but wasn't an option.

'I think I'm going to have to buy lollies today, Dawn. A sugar rush is something to live for.'

Dawn's disapproving face softened.

'You pass by Dalefield Dairy, don't you? They have a good selection of pick-and-mix lollies. That dairy is still run by normal people.'

'As opposed to dastardly foreigners you mean?'

'Yes, ha ha.'

A week later, I was sorting next to Johnno. The millions of Contact Energy flyers with addresses on them had upset him.

'Outrageous! I don't mind useful work, but half of these are addressed to non-existent numbers. We're at the mercy of any marketing baboon wanting to send out junk mail! Less of this carry-on in the old days, they've ruined a good job here. I need to find another way to make money. What do you reckon if I get myself a Mr Whippy van, Ed?'

'Selling ice cream to kids? You could sideline in marijuana too.'

'Yeah ... you've thought about it before then?'

Did he know I was joking? Johnno didn't say anything for the next two hours. Conversations about various get-rich-quick schemes drifted over the cases. Same old stuff: the TAB, Lotto, or the casino. I half listened to them, half to The Cars, Pink Floyd, and Bowie on the radio. I didn't mind these artists. But the DJs played the same songs as yesterday. Same songs for thirty years. An easy job: commercial radio playlist put-togetherer. I sipped on bad instant coffee. The stuff made me fart, but you could blame someone else for the smell. In the juvenile atmosphere of the depot, respect was given to a ventriloquist farter.

When I got out to deliver, rain poured down. I had a ton of packages in my trailer and a million letters, not to mention those Contact Energy flyers. I had a signature item for an old bastard on Elgin Street. He wasn't home. That meant I had to leave a card to call in the mailbox, and they weren't easy to write out in the rain. The ones

I had in my pockets were soaked and so useless. Never mind. I always kept an emergency supply under the seat ... Cor, what a stench! And there it was! Resurrected from the dead. No doubt, it was the same sandwich. Such commitment, either Johnno or Dawn must have got it out of the bin. But that was a week ago! This was inspiring. What great colleagues.

5

The team didn't appreciate talking out of turn at morning briefs. All the posties would gather around perched on stools, resentful at having their sorting delayed or interrupted. They wanted to be done sorting and get out of the depot. Asking questions, giving advice, or raising irrelevant issues wasted time. Some things were important enough to be talked about, but you needed some experience to judge which. Ross, a relative newcomer, would've done well to keep a stoic silence. Yet this was beyond him. He couldn't keep his mouth shut, blurting out stuff like:

'Everybody be careful out there in the wind.'

'The other day I got a courier parcel so long I couldn't put it on my Kurrus. We need to do something about this, it's not on.'

'If we just keep talking to each other about these problems, everything will be okay.'

Innocuous stuff, but these utterances could be classified as talking out of turn. Some of the long-term posties grumbled, 'He's only been here three minutes and he already knows it all!'

Six foot when not stooping, the powerfully built Ross had square calves and a square head. His rather brutish appearance didn't suit his personality—he was a thinker. He stormed around the depot with great energy, a danger to the hinges of every door he flung open. Later he would admit to me racing around covered up his slacking.

HQ wanted to do away with bicycles nationwide because they couldn't hold enough parcels. Internet shopping meant an increase in parcels, while letter volumes kept falling. I started on the job four months after Ross, so I never got the pushbike experience. He claimed they didn't tell him about the Kurrus during the recruiting process, something he was bitter about. 'They bloody tricked me.' He'd liked the bikes.

I figured those who recruited him had no idea when the Kurrus revolution would be implemented. Most organisations operate on more of a need-to-know basis than we imagine. The strategic planners live in a bubble and don't announce anything until they bloody feel like it.

Ross took a liking to me after our brief conversation about rats. He'd greet me by the lockers or in the smoko room and tell me about the events of the previous day's delivery. We talked about aggressive dogs and non-existent houses. An intense character, a vein would pop out his forehead as he spoke.

'Imagine if that dog on Wills Street got near a kid!'

'Ten letters a week for that place and it's an empty section.'

He entered my personal space to utter these meaningful phrases. I had a genuine gripe against his space invasions because of his habit of eating raw garlic cloves. He swore they warded off any illness. It had to be raw garlic, cooking it took out a lot of the vitamin C and antioxidants. He cut the cloves up and put them in his pâté sandwiches. Too bad he couldn't pick up on his own bad breath. While devouring a tuna sandwich—my tuna breath wasn't that bad—in the smoko room, I heard Dawn and Joyce, real posties with decades of experience, talking about Ross.

'He's a weirdo!' Dawn said, summarising the opinion of many.

'Give credit where it's due—he is fast at sorting!'

'Yeah, but yesterday he came back with pants covered in mud. Saw him outside hosing himself down. Hate to think how he got that way. And have you seen him opening and shutting doors? Heck, we'll be replacing all the hinges soon. Anyway, you playing Lotto this weekend Joyce?'

'Yeah, sure will be … I've got a new system worked out.'

As fascinating as their tips on how to pick Lotto numbers were, I decided to cut my break short and get delivering. Out on my run, it was sunny, my concentration was good, and the public didn't put in too many appearances. I started to worry things were going too well. I told myself not to get too cocky and confident because something would go wrong. When I stepped in dog shit, it was almost a relief.

Because of the garlic, I preferred talking to Ross while we sorted. Two shelves full of letters between us kept the vampire-slaying smell at bay. One morning, while sorting at the case next to me, he asked me, 'Did you meet the union guy yesterday?'

'Yep.'

I had met Murray, the postal union rep, in the smoko room. He was around forty, with slicked-back hair and a crooked goatee. Dunking a biscuit in his tea, Murray told me he was investigating whether the company was streaming out packages weighing over twenty-five kilos. I said I thought they were, and van couriers got the heavy stuff. Murray looked disappointed, then smiled and said, 'I used to have a job where I lifted twenty-five kg slabs of butter all day long. You guys might have one or two heavy packages, but that was real hard work.'

I was prickly about listening to people's work stories during break time and this one reminded me of, 'When I was at school, we walked ten miles every morning through the snow and blah blah blah.' And did Murray see the contradiction in relating this anecdote? The hard work of lifting butter was a good thing, it had made him a man. But he wanted to jump on the company for the injustice of making us lift the occasional heavy package.

Ross had his own take on Murray and the union. 'These unions won't do anything, mate. It's all a political game to them. In their catered meetings with company bosses, they'll get a few small concessions for the workers. But it's hard to get tough when you're enjoying free sausage rolls and barista-made coffee, so they're good with what's happening.'

'And what is happening?'

'Classic worker exploitation mate. Caused by the purchase of those bloody ... ah ...'

'Kurrus?'

'Yes, those bloody machines. It's up to us, as the pilot depot, to stop them from spreading. There's a lot wrong with them ... can only go forty-five an hour, making them unsafe in the flow of traffic. They're unstable and the trailers are a nightmare. I could go on, but you know all this stuff. The company will go ahead and introduce them nationwide if we don't act. We need to say no and refuse to go out on them one day. What can they do? Nobody else is trained to drive them. They'll have to let us back on the push bikes.'

'I don't get how it's worker exploitation.'

'It's plain as day. The company invests in an upgrade of technological capital and makes the work more intense for labour—flogs the horses harder. Now we're on those machines, we have to concentrate on driving, and we deliver a whole range of different stuff, not just letters, but fucking golf bags and boxes of wine.'

I shrugged. The golf bags sounded like an exaggeration.

'Yeah ... but there isn't exactly a secondhand market for those Kurrus. They'll never let us off them, now they've forked out the cash. They're paying us by the hour for delivery too, so they aren't forcing us to go super quick. We have time for those extra tasks.'

'Not for long, the measurers are coming.'

A crashing noise came from the interchange—a forklift dropping a pallet. We paused our conversation to watch Mavis run out of her office dead keen to give the forklift driver a bollocking.

'The big boss himself will be here next month,' I said. 'Maybe you can talk to him about the Kurrus, Ross.' Notices informing us of the CEO's upcoming meeting with the depot staff had been plastered up by the lockers and in the smoko room. 'And maybe Murray will tell him what's what.'

'He'd better. If he doesn't, I might have to do something to sabotage these poisonous technological upgrades. That's what the Luddites did. Everybody thinks a Luddite is someone who can't use a computer, but that's not the case.'

'I know, Ross. The Luddite mission is to do away with technological innovations that make our lives worse. I don't think the Kurrus much of an innovation though. I'll be more impressed when they start using drones to deliver mail.'

Ross didn't continue the conversation. He wandered off grumbling to himself. He was fired up, but I was worried for him. The best thing to do? Help him to get a grip and tell him there were injustices, but you needed to bear them. He'd be better to do his work and keep quiet because the others wouldn't follow Ross in his planned Kurrus boycott. Tugging me the other way, was my desire to egg him on. His mission was futile but at least he brought some colour to proceedings. I knew he'd do something stupid soon … and I looked forward to it.

Another day, another team brief with Mavis. What a joy. Ross and I were admonished for damaging our trailers in minor crashes. This was the second time I'd managed to ding mine.

'The damage was minimal,' Ross said to me after the brief, 'and it's easy to lose control of those unsteady machines and tip the trailers. They won't allow us to make one mistake, it's ridiculous!'

I agreed. 'But look at what we are up against, mate!'

I referred to Dawn who never missorted and cleaned her vehicle every day. She wasn't going to ding her trailer. Ross went quiet. Over my case, I could see him fuming as he shoved letters into slots. He was planning something. He would have done well to remember that if he caused trouble he could be out of a job, especially if he wasn't a member of the union—which he wasn't. He'd be fucked. But what if he succeeded? Managed to organise the workers to stop riding the electric buggies and cause a return to the bikes, what then? He'd be our representative for life. And how would that go? Ross got most of his ideas from Marx, whose work I'd studied to a limited extent. I didn't show off this kind of knowledge, as I didn't want anybody around the depot to know I'd been to university. Mavis knew as she'd seen my CV—but she would have disliked me anyway, so it didn't matter. Ross, who had a destructive intellectual side, would have done well to remember Marx's assertion that dead generations weigh heavily once the revolution has begun. Meaning you inevitably morph into the monster you've overthrown. And so, Ross would have to start playing the political game like the others who came before him—such as Murray. This was the rubbish going through my brain as my arms, hands, and eyes continued sorting letters. I didn't think I could articulate my thoughts to Ross convincingly though.

A few days later, when I drove into the depot after delivery, some dude was whizzing around the interchange on a Kurrus. He asked me in accented, yet perfect English,

'Where do you park K571?' I didn't know. A Swiss engineer, he was fitting the machines with wider wheels to make them more stable. Not only new wheels for the Kurrus but the trailers too. The Kurrus in Switzerland didn't have trailers—they had been designed by a birdbrained Kiwi company. The Swiss engineers had burst out laughing when they first saw them.

Mavis updated us the next morning. With the aid of her gravelly throat and bad adenoids, she told us about the new wheels. 'The tests have had positive results; stability is much improved. No more damaged trailers. It'll be safer for you guys too, that's always been our priority. Look after those wheels, they've been flown in from Switzerland at great cost.'

Ross was triumphant when we returned to sorting. 'So, they *were* unsafe! As if they care about us. This is about looking after their image by not having any accidents reported on in the newspaper. But do you think they'll say sorry for bollocking us over our tipping those defective trailers?'

'No, I don't', I said. 'They'll justify it because you have to bollock somebody when things go wrong. If they say sorry it's like taking the bollocking back, and then they'll have to administer another one. Only the Kurrus delivery machines deserve it, but there'd be no satisfaction in bollocking them. And then how about this for ridiculous: Mavis won't even give me a new marker pen because she says it'd blow the stationary budget, and now thousands spent on the bloody wheels.'

Ross came round to my sorting case. Mr Garlic Breath was all smiles. He grabbed my hand and shook it vigorously. 'My God, is that anger? I didn't think you had it in you, Ed! Don't worry, if something goes wrong here, there'll always be a plan B. Don't be like the others, petrified of losing a job they don't like.'

6

Johnno didn't look comfortable standing with his bony back against the concrete wall, switching a disposable plastic cup of hot tea from hand to hand. Why hadn't he learnt to double-up cups?

'Drinking your tea in the interchange, Johnno?' I asked. 'Then again, sometimes I drink coffee on the toilet to avoid the chatter in the smoko room. I suppose that's worse.'

'That's disgusting, what's wrong with smoko room natter, you odd bod? I'm out here because there's extra work to pick up. Joyce is sick. Mavis always checks the smoko room, but maybe not out here.'

I shouldn't have told him about drinking coffee on the toilet. I didn't dwell on my mistake though.

'When's Joyce retiring?'

'Must be any day now. The old girl is healthy as a goat, but she's got a lot of sick leave owing. Good on her for taking it. Your mate Ross lectured her about smoking the other day, saying she should quit for her grandkids ...

self-righteous bastard. You need to tell him to keep his mouth shut.'

'I've got no control over him. Hey, you don't take breaks normally. What's changed, Mr. Finish-as-fast-as-possible?'

'Lost my motivation ever since I started painting my house. When I get home, I can't sit down and have a cuppa tea. I mean, I can, just can't enjoy it, knowing I'll have to start painting after.'

Mavis appeared over by the door that separated the sorting floor from the interchange. She spotted us, frowned, and strode over, swinging her arms with purpose.

'No escape, Johnny Boy. Mavis has found you,' I whispered.

Johnno's expression went from sullen to despairing.

'Johnno, since you're standing around with all the time in the world, you can pick up a portion of run thirteen. And take those bloody speakers off your Kurrus—they're a health and safety risk! I don't want anyone seeing them out there!'

Or hearing them, more like. Mavis left us, her black aura in tow. She'd got to me earlier, giving me some of run fifteen to do.

'Blimey, a ray of sunshine old sandpaper throat. No tunes for me out there anymore,' Johnno said, resigned to his fate.

'So, about this painting the house and taking breaks? I don't get it. I hope it's not too complicated. If you talk for too long in that Brummie accent, I'll get a headache.'

'Ha-dee-fucking ha. The sooner I go home, the sooner I have to start the bloody painting. And painting the house isn't like the mail, where there's a set amount for one day that's done when it's done. No, it feels endless. And when I finish painting the house, I know the wife will say it's time for new wallpaper. And you know what happens then?'

'No?'

'The worst part of marriage, mate. Find me a married man in the Western World who hasn't gone through this: having to decide on an off-white for the wallpaper, or bathroom tiles, or the ceiling. Off-white, it can't be any other colour. But they have hundreds of *off-whites*, all with silly names like *polar* or *paradise*. And none are quite right for the job.'

'Sounds like hell. At least you've worked out the meaning of taking a break: to relax because there is always more to do.'

'I take them now because the wife's got an eagle eye for what I've got done at home. It's never enough to justify a break.'

'She sounds, um, efficient.'

Johnno finished his tea, scrunched the plastic cup, and threw it. He missed the bin. Grumbling, he walked over to pick it up.

'You could get Dawn's husband to do your painting maybe? I heard he doesn't charge much.'

'Nah, mate. No way. Something seriously wrong with that one. You watch out for him. Dawn has got herself a ticking time bomb there.'

'What do you mean?'

'I'll say no more, not my place. But her husband's a nutter, worse than your mate Ross.'

I didn't want the conversation to end, so I changed the subject.

'Hey, doesn't Mavis piss you off? Why does she have to be so aggressive? It's all so personal to her. She could allocate extra work to people in a systematic way without getting upset about it.'

Johnno shrugged, 'Get used to it, most managers are that way.'

'I'm sick of it. I've got a good idea though.'

'Here we go.' He rolled his eyes.

'Rotating managers between cities. That way we only have to put up with the specific evils of any given over-lord for a limited time. I've never believed in the bet-ter-the-devil-you-know saying.'

'Impractical, mate. Cost inefficient and you know it. Don't worry, the Everywhere Spirit will get to Mavis in the end.'

'The Everywhere Spirit? You've lost me.'

'I'm talking about what happened to General Custer. You know who General Custer is, right?'

'Yeah, of course.'

'Right, well ... he attacked the Cheyenne Indians but later made friends and smoked the peace pipe with them. They warned him if he ever attacked them again, he'd have to reckon with the Everywhere Spirit. Of course, he did attack them again at Little Bighorn and got killed ... the Everywhere Spirit made sure of it. The Cheyenne women pierced his corpse's ears with needles to help him hear better in the afterlife, as in this world he had been deaf.

Mavis is like Custer in that she's had a fair number of conflicts over the years. So far, her aggression has got her through, but one day she'll get hers.'

'I didn't know they taught American history so well in Birmingham. I'm not sure I want such a violent end for Mavis.'

'Yeah mate, you do. But don't try to get revenge yourself. Let it happen organically. And I'm not from Birmingham. I'm from Dudley. They didn't teach me about Custer at school. My parents used to work late and didn't have anybody to look after me, so I went to the library after school. I read about General Custer there. Getting a book smart my Dad used to say. He meant that as an insult. What did he expect, though? Did he want me to play tiddlywinks in the library? Never made my boy stay in the library alone. He can barely read but working as a builder he makes more than I ever will. Funny how things work out, Ed. I better get bloody going, this mail isn't going to deliver itself.'

I hadn't reckoned on Johnno having this philosophical side. I still didn't want the conversation to end. 'I like your resignation about things. Leave things to supernatural powers, and they'll sort it out.'

He smirked. 'You're taking the piss out of me, Ed. Well, we can't all be action men like your mate Ross. Patience, that's the way.'

'Except when it comes to getting your round done …'

'Yeah, I used to be quick at that, before this house painting. Do me a favour, go in and tell Mavis I'll come back for the run thirteen mail. I've got a full load here, trailer and all.'

Off Johnno went, his knees sticking out of either side of his Kurrus. I searched for the one air pump that worked. After filling my tyres, I needed to talk to my favourite person, General Mavis Custer. In her office, she had her head in her hands and elbows resting on the desk. She didn't take pressure well, our Mavis. What had happened to upset her? Head Office wasn't liking some of the stats she'd sent in perhaps? Had we done something to stuff up her bonus? She looked pathetic. Could I get a concession out of her in this vulnerable state? We all wanted poly-styrene disposable cups that would shield our hands from the heat of boiling drinks, unlike the thin plastic ones we had now. I could ask for those. What would she say? 'Bring your own bloody cup in!' or, 'We haven't got time to drink coffee around here!' Attack, attack—that was her style. She would never take up the peace pipe or heed warnings about the Everywhere Spirit.

'Johnno's coming back to pick up his share of run thir-teen.'

She looked up. Her eyes were red, and her facial wrin-kles looked deeper than usual. I tensed for a burst of toxicity. It didn't happen.

'That's fine, thanks for letting me know.'

'OK, you're welcome.' I turned and walked out of her office.

'Pssst,' Dawn gave me the raised eyebrows from her sorting case.

'What's up?'

'Mavis's brother broke his restraining order.' Nearly choking with excitement, Dawn pulled a piece of news-paper out of her pocket and unfolded it.

'Have a gawk at this.'

I took it and read.

A man who approached his former partner with a meat cleaver appeared in the district court yesterday and was sentenced to six months in prison. Rodney Ledger admitted knocking on the door of his ex's residence despite a restraining order. The woman opened the door, and he began verbally abusing her. When her current partner came to see what was happening, Ledger knocked the man down. A butcher by trade, Ledger then went to his van and returned with a meat cleaver. At this stage, police reached the scene. The judge said Ledger was seconds away from committing an act of violence that could have caused grievous bodily harm.

'Wow, he sounds murderous.'

'Go easy on her for a bit, Ed. She's upset.'

'So, that's why Mavis left early yesterday, to attend the court case. Looks like aggression runs in the Ledger family. Did you rip this out of the smoko room paper? Are you trying to hide it from the rest?'

'No, I don't care who finds out. I bought my own paper because I was so excited about the story.'

Johnno and his Everywhere Spirit had made me feel more able to cope with Mavis. However, Dawn's newspaper story made me even more terrified of her than before.

7

The time had come for our delivery runs to be re-measured. Norm arrived at our small depot to do this. He'd been promoted from doing inductions at HQ in Wellington. His new title was Nationwide Manager of Measuring.

Mavis gave us the lowdown on Norm's mission. 'He doesn't need to measure all the postie runs, just a few so he can update the system to take account of how long delivery takes with the Kurrus machines. There's some stuff you can do on them you couldn't on the bikes and vice versa. The sooner we get this done, the sooner you can be paid per item on your runs and fast workers will get what they deserve, and slow coaches can stop milking the system. Do I have any volunteers? Come on, it's always the same people putting their hands up and I'm bloody sick of it.'

Mavis's guilt trip worked on me, not that I wanted to please her, but she was right: the same characters—usually

Dawn and Joyce—volunteered for annoying tasks. Out of a misguided sense of guilt, I volunteered to be followed.

I liked the guy, but I was apprehensive about Norm following me. To get an accurate and fair measurement, you should deliver at normal speed. The measurer wasn't meant to push, but Norm with his army background couldn't help demanding speed.

Norm, his chest and arms bursting out of a yellow and red postie shirt, stood next to me in the interchange holding a clipboard. 'I'm going to start loading up,' I told him. 'I won't need the trailer today ... not too many big parcels, reckon I can squeeze everything in the back of the Kurrus.'

'That happen often?'

'No, hardly ever.' I lied because I didn't want him to report to HQ any underutilisation of the expensive vehicles. Norm should've understood Tuesday was the lightest day of the week, but never having been a postie maybe he didn't.

'OK now for the safety check.'

'You do this every day, eh?'

'Yes, indeed.' I looked at the check sheet. Blow me if I hadn't checked off Monday's boxes. I made a great show of testing the horn, the brakes and tyre pressure. Hopefully, he didn't notice I checked off two days at once. While Norm did the safety check on the spare Kurrus he'd be using, I wolfed down a can of tuna by the lockers.

Out on delivery, having Norm behind me was oppressive. I couldn't let my mind drift like usual. I felt imprisoned by his hundred per cent focus on the job. Whenever I got off the Kurrus to run to a letter box, I glanced back at him and saw him furiously writing on his clipboard. He had a lot to record: footpaths too narrow for the Kurrus, places one had to dismount to reach a letterbox, long driveways, the number of letterboxes in a cluster outside some dingy flats, etc. etc. ad infinitum.

My second day with Norm turned out like the first: draining. That evening, I felt dead tired and went to bed two hours earlier than normal. The next day, a Thursday, Norm followed Johnno. I don't know whether Johnno had volunteered, or Mavis had selected him for this honour, but in any case, I was happy to have time off from Norm. Johnno's run was extra hilly and would give Norm some good variation for his data sample.

Johnno gave me his cutting opinion of the National Manager of Measuring: 'Blimey, Soldier Boy is a pain! Can't wait to get rid of him.'

'We're on the same page, Johnno.'

By contrast, Norm was happy spending time with us, 'I'll keep alternating between Johnno and yourself. I want to get some low- and high-volume days, some good and bad weather.'

On my third day with Norm, an opportunity presented itself down Oak Grove. Something to break up the rhythm of the day. A yappy little dog had tried to bolt past me the last time I opened the gate at number nine. This time I accidentally on purpose let the runt of a dog out onto the street.

'Shit, didn't see that coming. Imagine if it gets run over.'

'After it!' Shouted Norm, a man always ready for action.

We gave pursuit. A speedy long-legged rat, the dog ran into the front garden at number twenty-four. We parked our Kurrus and continued on foot, through the front garden and down the gravel path at the side of the house. The back garden was a large expanse of uncut lawn. The mutt flew across the grass and through a gap in the back fence. Damn badly maintained place. I managed to rip my work-issued MC Hammer-style pants scrambling over the fence. These pants had protective padding in case we fell off our Kurrus, but they were uncomfortable and heavy. Head office hadn't given the okay for us to wear shorts yet. They were still mulling over the paperwork. Norm, who hadn't been issued Hammer pants, athletically bolted over the fence. We found ourselves in another back garden, this time with a well-cut lawn. Neither the dog nor the residents appeared. 'I'll call Mavis and report a lost dog—we can't spend all day trying to find it.' I was going to get a bollocking, and this time I deserved it. I slumped down on a rickety piece of garden furniture. So did Norm.

'Better call a bloody helicopter to search for that pooch,' Norm said.

I laughed long and loud, partly because I thought the joke funny and partly to ingratiate myself. Before I'd finished cackling the dog reappeared. With us sitting down, he was less spooked. I took a gingernut out of my pocket and tempted him with it. Slowly he approached. When I grabbed him by the collar he didn't bite. What a result! I'd got a joke from Norm and now had no bollocking from Mavis to worry about. As we walked back to our Kurrus, Norm slapped me on the back. 'Nice work. I could see your heart was in the chase. Mission accomplished—and just as well because a missing dog is always a bad look. People are crazy about their pets. I reckon you could've been a decent soldier, Ed'

What a compliment. I doubted he meant it, but after sharing an adventure I felt we'd become mates. Norm reinforced this notion by saying, 'Once we're done today let's have a beer at my hotel. On the company credit card of course.'

He didn't phrase it as a question: my accepting the invitation was a given. Everything flowed for the rest of the delivery run. I felt energetic and didn't miss a single mailbox. Norm's questions and note-taking didn't seem as oppressive as before. We got back to the depot early.

'Mate, I'll meet you in the car park in ten minutes. I'm parked next to your little Nissan, mine's the black SUV.'

'Ok, Norm.' A black SUV of course.

He strode off towards the sorting floor, leaving me to unload undelivered packages and write up my docket. I needed to hurry if I didn't want to keep him waiting. Along with the interchange area's usual musty and metallic odours, I detected stale sweat in the air. Who'd left that behind? Most of the crew, even Ross, came daily in clean polyester shirts. In case someone was watching, I checked my underarms surreptitiously by reaching up to scratch the back of my head. I could then turn my head to the side to get a whiff of my armpit. Nothing. Then I noticed that the steel mesh cages used for transporting courier parcels had been taken away. The mystery was solved. The sweaty smell had been left behind by the truck driver who looked like a walrus and came daily to pick up the cages.

Distractions, distractions ... Norm would be waiting for me outside. But when I entered the sorting floor, I spotted him through the open door of Mavis's office. Twenty minutes later, I was still sitting in my Nissan watching stray cats clean themselves and listening to Blue Öyster Cult. Finally, Norm tapped on my window.

'Pity you need to take your car to the hotel and can't ride with me, Ed. This company Mitsubishi is new, and the leather seats smell great. Got a kick-arse engine too—nothing like what I used to drive in Iraq—but the locals are less hostile here. Anyway, the hotel is called The Manor—you'll follow me—but I'm giving you the name in case you can't keep up.' He punched me lightly on the shoulder and turned to get in his SUV. His wheels screeched as he pulled out of the car park. He accelerated up the road Ferrari-like, but I caught up at the red light fifty metres on. Predictable, I thought, he's showing off. The rest of the trip took us through suburbia sans traffic lights, but Norm slowed down slightly, and so I managed to keep his black SUV in sight.

A beautiful Edwardian mansion, The Manor badly needed a coat of paint. We parked in the tarmacked-over area that must've once been a nice front garden.

In the lobby, Norm said, 'Take a pew here mate,' gesturing to an armchair. 'I've got to get out of this horrible polyester shirt. I'll head up to my room and be back down in a tick.'

'No worries.' I preferred waiting in the lobby to going upstairs to see his muscles. In a flasher hotel, I might've been self-conscious wearing my postie uniform but not here. From the outside, The Manor was all faded architectural glory. Inside, the unadorned off-white wallpaper and beige carpet didn't inspire.

Improving the colour palette of this scene, Norm reappeared in a marine blue Lacoste polo shirt. I reckoned he'd bought medium instead of large to make his muscles pop.

Keen to get a cold beer, I asked, 'Where's the bar?'

'There isn't one, we order drinks at reception. Not the greatest, is it? I'm trying to get a better accommodation allowance. With a few extra bucks, I could stay at the Novotel instead of this ten-room dump. Post needs to work harder to retain their staff.'

'Where are you based, Norm?'

'My place is in Hastings.'

'But you still do the training sessions for new posties in Wellington in addition to measuring all around the place?'

'Yeah, they don't even fly me. I have to drive.'

In a company car and with a company credit card for expenses. I wanted to say something but bit my tongue.

An unforgiving white light, powerful enough to show up pimples you never knew you had, hung directly above the reception desk. That bulb was more suited to a hospital than a hotel. To combat the glare, the woman on duty wore dark glasses.

'How's things?' I asked after we approached the desk. It was hard to tell whether she'd seen us or not. And perhaps she hadn't heard us either; I saw no sign of ears under her thick, waist-length, black hair.

She turned her shades my way and said, 'Not so good.'

A refreshing answer in this world filled with people trying to convince others of their happiness.

'What's happened?' asked Norm. He picked the drinks list off the counter and handed it to me.

'Some guests left without paying this morning: a couple and their kid. With a child involved, we cut them some slack. Bloody fat Māori women said they'd have the money today. Eleven nights they stayed. We're looking after this place for our friends—the owners—who are on a cruise. They'll be right pissed off when they hear about this.'

'What about the videotape? You've got a camera.' Norm pointed to the wall behind reception. 'What did the husband look like? Could you ID him too?' Norm's eyes shone; security was one of his areas of expertise.

I scanned the drinks list of six items: Steinlager, Export Gold, Speights Ale, Tui, Coke, and Sprite.

'We've looked at the videotape, and you can see their faces clearly, but the police don't want to come and look at it.'

'Useless, eh!'

'Yes, useless. The husband looked like a heavy metal guitarist. A skinny white guy with long hair dressed in black denim. What bloody con artists.'

'Sorry to hear this happened to you. What do you want, Ed?'

'A Steinlager.'

'Same for me.'

The woman took off her dark glasses, turned around and bent down to open a small beer fridge. She placed the bottles on the counter, took a lighter out of her pocket, and deftly used it to open the two bottles.

'Here, I'll pay now,' Norm said, brandishing his credit card.

'Don't worry, we can put them on your room.'

'Nah, on my card is better.'

'That's twelve dollars then,' she said, picking up the EFTPOS machine.

Not a bad price, I thought as Norm swiped his card and punched in his pin.

Beers in hand, we walked across the lobby to the fake leather armchairs.

'Cheers, mate.' I said, and we clinked bottles.

'Bloody racist that woman.' I looked nervously towards reception after Norm said this, but the woman had disappeared into the room behind reception.

'Did you hear her? Fat Māori lady,' she said. 'And she herself has got some Māori in her. She's probably thinking I'm a black bastard who's going to take off without paying too. That's why I paid on the spot for the beers. I think that showed her how I felt.'

'Too subtle, I'd say.'

'Yeah, you're right. She doesn't look like the most intuitive type and what's with those glasses? You get the next beers. I don't want to talk to her right now. Tell her room 205.'

He'd already downed his Steinlager, so I followed suit. When I stood up, Norm gave me a once-over.

'Geez mate ... one more beer for you only. Got a pot belly going on there. Delivering mail on a bike would've been good for you.'

In saying this he reestablished his alpha status. I'd diminished it by calling his move to pay upfront for his beers too subtle. Being subtle was not an alpha trait. He needed to reestablish the hierarchy. He didn't want me getting too close to him. It's strange but Alphas are delicate—they need everything to go their way.

I rang the bell at reception and the woman emerged from out back.

'Two more Steinlagers, please. Put them on room 205.'

She frowned. I guessed she didn't like the hassle of taking her glasses off to get beers out of the fridge. Oddly, she had no problem working the reception computer in her dark glasses.

'Room 205 ... and your name was?'

'Um ... Norman.'

'Last name?'

'I'll check, it's my mate who's staying here.'

'Don't bother, I've put two Steinlagers on room 205 under the name Norman.' She was satisfied that she'd made the transaction more difficult than necessary.

Before I could get my bum down on the armchair, Norm began talking. 'Like I said, riding a bike would do you good. I like bikes. They're flexible and reliable. That's what you want in a tight spot, a contraption that's helped humans out for centuries or at least decades. You know what my favourite piece of equipment in Iraq was?'

'Swiss army knife?'

'No—a Fulton angle-head flashlight. The power went out all the time over there and that torch lasted for months on one set of batteries so I could always read.'

'What did you read?'

'Caesar, Patton, Hannibal ... books great generals wrote about their campaigns.'

'I didn't know Hannibal wrote a book.'

Norm gave me a sharp look and changed the subject.

'Do you know the most efficient way to deliver mail going forward?

I decided to let him take control of this one. 'No, I don't.'

'In five years, all mail will be delivered by vans, no Kurrus, no bikes, no posties, and certainly no drones. The market will find the most efficient option despite whatever the drongos in charge want. These Kurrus are a fad. I bet you've heard others say they'll be around a long time because Post has invested so much. I disagree. Post will sell them as mobility scooters. Lots of oldies will be willing to pay a good price. I'm having fun going out on the Kurrus with you and Johnno ... but I don't have to deliver mail on them six days a week. I know that's tedious. But don't worry, stick to this job and you'll be driving a van soon.'

I nodded. People loved giving their opinions on the Swiss vehicles. I didn't agree with Norm, I thought drone delivery was a real possibility.

'Will people get a fair rate based on your measurements?' I asked.

'Come on mate, you know that a fair rate is impossible to define. Don't ask silly questions.'

Norm drained the rest of his beer.

'Right, I'm going to my room. Make sure that's your last. We don't want you drink driving or extending that waistline further.'

'Thanks for the beers.'

'No worries.'

I still had half my beer left. Alone, I felt self-conscious drinking alcohol in my postie uniform. But why? Apart from the receptionist in shades, The Manor appeared to be deserted.

8

It was all action in the smoko room. Dawn buttered a muffin and Johnno sipped tea. At another table, Joyce hogged the newspaper and drank from a giant green can. Surely, people in their sixties shouldn't consume energy drinks. I sat down next to Ross at a third table. He unwrapped a pie. A couple of seconds later, half the pie was gone.

'Don't burn your throat with the hot mince, mate,' I said.

'Looks like a bloody pelican.' Dawn had stopped her buttering to stare at Ross eating. Johnno, too, was transfixed and held his mug suspended halfway to his mouth. 'Bloody hell, finished it in five seconds.'

The pie-eating show was over before it began, and Dawn returned to bending Johnno's ear.

'When is this measurer fellow going to finish up and publish his results? I'm sick of being paid by the hour.'

'I don't know. We need to get used to these Kurrus—no hurry to get back to a piece rate.'

Johnno's new go-slow policy wasn't as innocent as he'd made out. The longer your delivery took, the more you got paid. But Johnno had only just slowed down? Why hadn't he done it from day one on the Kurrus? Well, he'd enjoyed having bragging rights for finishing first. Also, after years of doing something as fast as you can, slowing down is difficult. But now Johnno had to go home and paint the house, it was worth getting paid to dawdle at work.

Dawn continued grumbling, we'd all heard it all before: 'If you're a fast deliverer, you should be rewarded, not the other way around. With this system, the slackers are winning. It's a disgrace.'

Johnno scoffed. This time he'd lost patience with her.

Ross piped up: 'Is anybody milking it by arriving back at the depot at six in the evening on a light mail day, Dawn? No, and Mavis wouldn't allow it. She's keeping tabs. And many of us are doing a better job now we aren't going hell for leather. Oh, I know you're conscientious Dawn, but some posties delivered the mail any which way to get the day done. And why did they do that? Did you feel the piece rate they paid us on the bikes was fair? No, not even Johnno could finish in a time that gave him a decent hourly wage.'

'No, but I bloody tried.'

'We know you did, Johnno. And what if the occasional person takes a twenty-minute break? That's costing the country less than our CEO Aitken's Cayman Island tax haven money.'

Dawn and Johnno nodded, attentive and quiet. It amazed me to see Ross making progress with them. But at the same time, I knew he'd lose them soon enough.

'Do you guys remember on the bikes we had everything on our runs timed down to the last second? It's not healthy for your day to be compartmentalised into tasks. This kind of scientific management takes the initiative away from the worker and breaks their work into a series of meaningless robotic chores. You're told how to sort your mail, how to load your bike, and how often to pump your tyres ...'

Joyce slipped away during this speech and now Dawn and Johnno stood up.

'Thanks for the analysis, Ross, but I'm outta here,' Johnno said.

'Me too,' said Dawn. 'You talk some crap, Ross. You say you want the bikes back and now you don't. I think you need your head read.'

'That's not what I'm saying—I want the bikes back and to be paid hourly.'

'See ya later, dreamer. I haven't got time for this. I haven't even finished my sorting.'

'Bloody hell, Dawn, why'd you take a break then?'

'To enjoy your wonderful company, Johnno.'

'Fuck off.'

Finally, Dawn and Johnno left, and Ross and I could talk. In me, Ross had a more patient audience. He could risk getting more theoretical.

'You heard of Frederick Taylor, Ed?'

'Maybe, did he have something to do with Henry Ford?' I had a vague idea of Taylor from a history paper I'd done that covered Detroit's car industry. I took another sip of instant coffee, hoping the caffeine would help me remember. Ross filled me in:

'Like Ford, Taylor was a nutbar, a menace to his fellow humans. He came up with the idea of scientific management. Under his system, workers who completed all tasks fast enough got a certain piece rate, and the slower ones got a lower rate. We don't have the lower and higher rates, only a warning if you're too slow ... still, our system of work is based on Taylor's ideas.'

'So, what's wrong with Taylor?'

'In his scientific management system, they don't take into account things like fatigue. No, the worker is treated as a machine. A machine shouldn't get tired, let alone have emotional ups and downs. They also tell you exactly how to do things. There's no room for individuals like Joyce who learnt her own way to be fast at sorting and delivering mail. Scientific management does nothing for morale. Concentrating only on efficiency leads to low staff retention, and that ultimately costs the company more than workers who—for example—pull their letters off the sorting case a little slow.'

'How long have you been preparing this speech?'

I expected Ross to give me a little smile, an acknowledgement of what a smarty-pants he was, but no, he continued in a serious vein.

'Safety, that's another problem when you push for speed on the Kurrus. But you know what really gets me? Management doesn't have to work under the same yoke. Nobody's measuring their emails-an-hour rate.'

'Their work is more abstract; you can't quantify everything.'

'You love making excuses for them don't you, Ed? Management, I mean.'

His one-man-stand for the workers entertained me. I had reservations about his reading of things though.

'They must move forward somehow, Ross, no matter how clumsy. Once upon a time posties rode around on bikes with a satchel of letters and chatted with retirees. Maybe you can find some way to make them take a step backwards, but it'll only be a temporary blip in their march forward to implementing the Kurrus nationwide. Further down the track, they'll do away with posties altogether. Only van couriers will survive. Or maybe all mail and packages will be delivered by drone. I'm not sure. Anyway, do you see yourself doing this job in two years?'

'No, you're right. I'll be somewhere else, dealing with the same kinds of problems.' Ross said with a grin.

9

Norm got up in front of the group to update us about the measuring. His immaculately ironed shirt struggled to contain his broad shoulders, and his shoes shone like black glass. Why did he bother looking so smart for us? The takeaway flat white coffee he sipped interested me more than his sartorial choices. I felt envious that he'd had time to slip out to a café.

Loving being up in front of a captive audience, Norm took twenty minutes to explain that he had the data he needed. The boffins at HQ would process it and soon we'd be on a piece rate when delivering. Ross's long-dead nemesis Frederick Taylor would've loved this.

'No more measuring, I'm going to enjoy my break today and it's sunny outside, too,' Johnno said as we walked into the smoko room. I made my coffee, Johnno his tea. Dawn was there as well, reading the paper. 'Have a look at this,' she shouted, making us jump. It was an article about drones being trialled to deliver mail in Singapore.

'Yeah, I'm not too worried about those,' I said. 'We'll be on universal income by the time drone delivery comes in. With our basic needs taken care of by the government, we can sit back, relax, and wait for the drones to deliver Chinese-made fake Rolexes to our doors.'

'Ha, you naive bugger,' Johnno said.

'What flavour is the muffin, Dawn?' I asked.

'Raspberry and cream cheese, not bad—got it at the Cambodian bakery. Much better than the tucker-truck muffins.'

'I dunno about a universal income. I can't see that happening. But I reckon those drones are a long way off in New Zealand anyway,' said Johnno. 'The more immediate plan is to fire the lot of us and bring in immigrants to work under worse conditions. They'll want the workers out on Sundays delivering Amazon packages. Did you know that those poor Yank mailmen are already doing it?'

'Hang on, what kind of immigrants?' Dawn asked. 'Poms like you?'

'No, Indians most likely. The good thing is the Tucker-truck Lady won't have much luck selling mouldy sandwiches to them. And she, not being a Pom like me, doesn't know how to cook curry. Her tucker truck will be put out of business by my curry truck, ha ha.'

Dawn arched her severely plucked dark eyebrows which didn't match her red hair. Her face said, 'What a lot of crap, Johnno,' but her mouth remained shut.

A week after Norm left, the Tucker-truck Lady came into the depot looking for him. He'd left an unpaid bill. The Tucker-truck lady was a stern woman with a face as lopsided as a cubist painting and shoulders wider than

Norm's. Every morning at ten, she pulled into the car park and tooted her horn; she sold rather stale sandwiches, pies, and fizzy drinks. Most of us were afraid of her. I for one never let my tab get above ten dollars. She demanded Norm's contact details from Mavis.

'Sorry, can't disclose those to a member of the public.'

It amused me to see those two face off and shake their fists at each other. Norm would be in the shit if he got sent back to us to do more measuring. He'd run up a tab of $37.50. His time in Iraq might have been preparation enough to deal with the Tucker-truck Lady's anger but I wasn't sure.

When Johnno heard about the unpaid bill, his opinion of Norm improved. 'He was okay, that Norm. Obsessed with speed and precision but you can't fault a fella for that.'

'Okay, I have to know, what have you got against the Tucker-truck Lady?' Dawn asked.

Johnno laughed, got up, chucked the remaining half of his cup of tea into the sink, and headed out to the interchange.

'If you want to find out I guess you need to follow him, Dawn,' I said.

'Screw that, I haven't finished my morning tea,' she said, stuffing her mouth with muffin. 'Here's your weirdo boyfriend, Ed. Looks like he wants to talk to you.'

Ross had appeared in the doorway. Something was on his mind. He gave me an eyebrow raise, and I followed him out to the lockers. I felt conspiratorial. I caught a whiff of garlic on his breath.

'You know the CEO will be here next month, right Ed?'

'What do you think he'll talk about?'

Ross screwed up his face at the stupidity of my question. 'Come on, Ed! We know the bastard CEO will lecture us about technology as a blessing to be embraced. The great lie ... he's gambling technology can make Post more efficient and turn greater profits in the short term because he wants a big bonus.'

I liked seeing this energy, this passion. But as Ross talked to me in the tight corridor by the lockers, his pacing made me nervous. He reminded me of two polar bears I'd seen at the zoo twenty years back. They paced back and forth in their enclosure, swinging their heads the exact same way every time they turned. The saddest inmates at a zoo, the yellow coats and the mania of the polar bears had traumatised the twelve-year-old me.

Ross continued pacing and talking about the Kurrus, drones, the exploitation of the workers, and the useless-ness of the union. I got overwhelmed and tuned out. I could sense a welcome break in routine coming, though. Ross was ready to act. With the CEO visiting, he had to do something. Could he get us off the Kurrus somehow? Even for a few days. If he could do this, he'd prove himself a Luddite warrior.

After Ross had first mentioned the Luddites, I'd cast my mind back to what I'd learnt about them at school. I remembered them as contemporaries of the Troglodytes in antiquity, with both groups living in caves. The Trogs were cave dwellers because of their innate primitiveness and the Luddites by choice. When technological innova-tions from Greece, like the alarm clock and coin money arrived, the Luddites saw unwelcome changes in society. The alarm clock broke people's reliance on their internal diurnal clock and therefore their connection with nature. Hoarding wealth had come about with the advent of agriculture and the storing of grain, but coins made matters much worse. To protest these changes, the Luddites joined the Troglodytes in caves. But this interesting, to me at least, history of the Luddites was of my own invention.

I had the basic idea right, but the timeframe all wrong. Only in my imagination did the Luddites hang out with the Trogs and the Greeks. When I had a spare couple of minutes, I googled the Luddites and found out what I'd got wrong.

The real story was that in nineteenth-century England, disgruntled workers went on a rampage and destroyed a bunch of stocking frames. These stocking frames were mechanical knitting machines that allowed factory bosses to fire skilled textile workers who demanded high wages.

The frames weren't cutting-edge technology; the Luddites had got their name from an earlier figure. Ned Ludd had smashed up a couple of stocking frames way back in the eighteenth century.

Ross would've done well to look at what became of the Luddite rebellion. The Luddites had organisation and commitment and clashed with the British army several times. But it was a losing battle in the long run. The Ludds got shot, hanged, imprisoned, or shipped off to Australia; a famous chapter in the history of the hopeless struggle to stop technological advancement in the workplace.

10

Like Dawn, I was curious about what Johnno had against the Tucker-truck Lady. I asked him, but he wouldn't say. However, it didn't take a genius to see she was a difficult character. And soon enough she caused me some trouble.

One evening at home, I saw an item on the news about small business owners working themselves to exhaustion. The story made me realise that the Tucker-truck Lady had contributed to two conflicts I'd had delivering mail that day.

I didn't normally watch the news, but Rachel was away for a few days and having the run of the flat, I decided to turn on the TV rather than stay glued to my laptop.

That morning, Mavis had given me part of run three to sort and deliver. As we sorted, a violent wind made the building shudder. Mavis walked around telling the posties to be careful out there because the forecast promised violent winds. 'Watch out for branches and other flying debris … don't corner too fast. We want you all back here in one piece.' Despite the caring message, her tone sounded more accusatory than motherly.

The wind warranted the warning, the streets were littered with fallen branches. Three minutes after leaving the depot, a flying object hit me in the face causing a sharp pain. I put my hand to my cheek, and it was wet with blood. Bad luck. The offending item had already blown twenty metres down the road but before impact, I'd caught a glimpse of a house for sale sign featuring a smiling, dark-haired woman standing in front of a white house. A vicious gust had made the corrugated plastic sign turn and accelerate so that the corner rammed into my cheek. Like when I'd cut my hand on a letterbox, my first concern was to make sure no blood dripped onto the mail. So, after touching my face, I wiped my hands thoroughly on my shorts.

My section of run three started a kilometre away from the depot, on a street that stained suburbia with its commercial feel. First up, I had a heavy package for a mechanic. It made metallic noises when I picked it up. I'd delivered packages to the behemoth who owned the mechanical workshop twice before and he'd received them with grease-encrusted, calloused hands—mitts to be proud of, unlike my soft, unskilled postie hands. He didn't look at me or say thank you. That he didn't want to give me the time of day didn't bother me. I just wanted to get away from him.

The heavy metal package was a signature item.

'Sign here, please.'

Instead of taking the scanner from me, he opened the package and took out a couple of metal car parts I didn't recognise.

'You're supposed to sign before opening.'

'That fucking stupid,' he growled, inspecting the parts with those hard, dextrous hands. 'What if they sent the wrong things?'

'Then you send them back to them.'

'No, I give them back to you.'

'That's not how it works.'

'What did you fucking say?' Straightening his back so he reached his full height of six-five, he looked at me for the first time. Inspecting me, surprise showed in his eyes. I must've looked demented. I hadn't bothered to clean up my cut check. I could feel blood running down my neck and pooling at my collar bone. He recovered quickly:

'If I get the wrong part off you, you'll fucking take it back.'

'Piss off,' I said and walked out. I wished Norm, Ross, or Johnno had been there to see me. I was so proud of myself, but my joy didn't last long.

As I walked into the carpet business next door, a bell rang as I triggered the sensor, and a wave of sweet perfume hit me even before the receptionist appeared at the front desk. She usually asked, 'Busy day today?' in a tone that indicated genuine interest. Anything she said in her Afrikaans accent made me happy because it reminded me of how it threw some of the other posties. Johnno had once proclaimed that the Russian lady on run three was lovely.

'Yeah, too right,' Joyce had replied. 'Can't understand a word bloody Svetlana says but she's given me lollies many times.'

'Svetlana' wasn't giving out lollies today.

'It's twelve-bloody-thirty,' she growled. 'I've been tracking that package. You scanned as out to deliver at seven this morning.'

'I scan my packages when I receive them, but then I've got to sort the mail,' I explained. 'And this part of town is extra for me today. I've only done it a couple of times before, so it took me a while to sort. I had to do my regular mail too.'

'Useless!' Svetlana didn't want to see reason. The problem with the Mechanic hadn't surprised me but Svetlana's heel turn didn't make any sense. Was she bipolar? I held the package out to her with a couple of letters.

'Look at you—you're covered in blood. Don't you know that's a disease risk? No, I don't want those letters. Take them away. Leave the package on the counter. Don't you watch rugby? What happens when a player starts bleeding? They go to the blood bin and get cleaned up. Otherwise, they might infect the other players with something.'

Svetlana talking about Rugby? I could tell Johnno and Joyce about this as proof she was South African not Russian. I unzipped a pocket and took my cell phone out. I fumbled around trying to find the voice recorder.

'Can you say that again, please.'

'What?'

'The stuff about rugby.'

'Are you recording me? Record this ... This postie had the nerve to try and give me mail covered in blood. I can't believe it.'

Although I hadn't cleaned my cheek or neck, I'd kept the letters clean. Svetlana was complaining about nothing.

I didn't expect any bad vibes at the Great Indian Spice Warehouse. Nevertheless, I walked in there weary and wary.

'Are you OK, my man?' The guy working there asked me. He looked at me over his reading glasses, which made him look kindly. I breathed deeply hoping the spices would overpower Svetlana's perfume which had lodged deep in my nose.

'Yes, fine. Not as bad as it looks.'

'Here.' He produced a pack of wet wipes from under the counter. I took a couple and cleaned my face.

'You must have some of our star anise.'

'What's that when it's at home?' I should have said no thanks and left. A neutral end. No problems. But I desperately wanted a positive interaction.

'A wonderful spice. Protects from free radicals and from inflammation. It'll keep your energy up. Perfect for you, my man, with that cut on your cheek and the wind today.'

'Can I take some of it now, dissolve it in water or something?'

'Well, no, it's a spice you'll need to cook with it.'

'You can dissolve turmeric in water.'

'Indeed you can. But this is different.'

He showed me a small plastic bag of what looked like tiny dried brown flowers.

'I'll take it.' I had to admire his business acumen, making a sales pitch to the postie.

'Would you like some turmeric too?'

'No thanks, I find it stains everything yellow.' No sooner had I said this than I wanted to put the words back in my mouth. Complaining about turmeric stains could be interpreted as being culturally insensitive. I tensed my jaw, waiting for his reaction ... but he only smiled and said, 'Have a good day, my man.'

The rest of the businesses on the street had mailboxes and no signature items so I didn't have to interact with anyone. Then I plunged back into suburbia. Almost done with run three, I found a box of *Roses Chocolates* in a letterbox with a yellow *Post-it* note with 'for postie' written on it. Postie in this case meant Joyce who was the regular on this run—but fuck it, it'd been a hard morning, and I still had my own run to deliver, so I ripped the box open. Never mind star anise, the chocolate boosted my energy. I imagined the solid relationship between Joyce and the people on her run. How did the mechanic treat her? Probably with respect.

I got home after five and flopped down in the lounge. The wind had given me a headache. I fished the bag of star anise out of my pocket. What could I cook with it? I had rice, onions, and frozen vegetables. I couldn't be bothered though. I settled on a can of tuna and two-minute noodles.

At twenty past six, I turned on the news and saw the story titled, 'Are small business owners working themselves to exhaustion?' which began with a reporter talking about a vehicle that hadn't moved when a traffic light turned green at a busy intersection.

'Cars drove around the truck honking loudly in annoyance, but nobody stopped to check on the driver.' So said a witness, a nervous man in his thirties with a bushy beard. This good Samaritan did pull over.

'I thought it might've been a medical incident. I videoed my intervention to protect myself. The driver has agreed for this video to be shown.'

Cut to the video the man took on his cell phone that showed the broad-shouldered Tucker-truck Lady asleep at the wheel of her truck. The good Samaritan could be heard asking her if she was okay. She didn't react. The man grabbed and shook her shoulder. She opened one eye at a time like a crocodile.

To my delight, an interview with the Tucker-truck Lady followed. The reporter asked her about the plight of a small business owner under current economic conditions.

'The government is killing us. They need to do something about the price of petrol, taxes, and all the bloody red tape if I want to hire somebody to help me out. I get up at three in the morning six days a week to make my fresh sandwiches and I don't get home until five in the evening. I'm doing seventy hours a week and barely breaking even.'

Whether the sandwiches she sold were always made on the same day was a moot point, but sure, she worked hard.

The reporter didn't shy away from the obvious tough question: 'If you're so tired that you fall asleep at a traffic light, aren't you a big danger to others? You could've easily caused an accident.'

'I've got to thank the young man who woke me up ... and he suggested something similar ... that I'm a danger to myself and others. He wants me to rest. Since he's such a nice young man, I've agreed to take a day off tomorrow. Just one day mind!'

Was the Tucker-truck Lady sweet on the bushy-beard-ed Samaritan?

As I watched the weather update—good news the wind would drop—an idea came to me that would allow me to rebuild the bridges burnt earlier in the day. I formulated a plan but was it worth carrying out? When I found myself having these kinds of doubts, I thought about an ex-girl-friend from back in university saying:

'You know what your problem is, Ed? You're too passive. And you never follow anything through.'

I'd show her! Although probably from her North Shore mansion the idea of a postman making sandwiches for people he delivered mail to would be baffling. Yes, that was my plan: to make sandwiches for the Mechanic and Svetlana. I gave up some of my treasured home alone time and headed to the supermarket.

What was the connection between the Tucker-truck Lady falling asleep at the wheel and my unpleasant inter-actions with the Mechanic and Svetlana? The commercial street on run three had no bakery and no dairy. Most of the businesses opened early. I guessed my two friends took lunch at twelve on the dot. And if they didn't bring lunch in themselves, they'd be beholden to the tucker truck for sustenance. So, their hunger had made them grumpy. If they hadn't watched the news, chances were they'd be expecting the tucker truck tomorrow. They'd be disappointed and hangry again—but I could save them. I didn't want to fall into racial stereotypes, but my guess was the guy at the Great Indian Spice Warehouse didn't rely on the tucker truck for his lunch.

When I returned from the supermarket, as an exception to the rule, I washed Rachel's dishes and wiped down the benchtop carefully. I took the largest chopping board off the shelf and assembled my ingredients. I couldn't make a tucker-truck range of sandwiches, so I calculated what kind of sandwich suited the intended devourer's personality. For the Mechanic, I buttered the bread and added three slices of roast beef and mild American mustard. He'd be okay with lettuce and tomato, but my other salad items, cucumber and alfa-alfa sprouts, seemed too fancy. I picked chicken and cranberry sauce for Svetlana but also made a vegetarian backup. It contained eggs, but I couldn't imagine her as a vegan. Then I started to second guess myself. What if the Mechanic only ate pies? Why embarrass myself? I put these doubts out of my mind. I was going ahead with my plan.

But what if Mavis didn't tap me on the shoulder for run three tomorrow because Joyce was back? Might happen but something told me that the fates wouldn't let me escape the rage of the Mechanic.

Sure enough, the next morning I found myself on the commercial street at twelve thirty with a package for the mechanic. This time I didn't have any blood on my cheek to distract him. I decided to deal with Svetlana first. I had a letter for her, but she wasn't sweating on a package.

'You again. When's Joyce back?' She said coldly.

'You hungry?' I said, almost gagging because it seemed she'd applied a double dose of *Red Moscow* aka the Soviet Chanel.

'What?'

'Are you hungry? Have you had your lunch?'

'No. No Joyce and no bloody tucker truck either.'

'I made you sandwiches.'

'What?'

'Do you like chicken and cranberry?' I placed a plastic container on the desk counter.

'Bloody hell! Thanks, I'm starving.'

'No worries.' Nothing else needed to be said. I walked out

Despite the success with Svetlana, I was trembling when I parked my Kurrus outside the workshop. Fear of mechanics was something genetic. I remembered my mother being stoked when I got my licence. That meant I could take her car to the workshop and so she wouldn't have to deal with any mechanics ... I held my breath and walked on in.

'It's you again you little bastard?'

I knew his tactic today would be to hand me back the items after opening the package. He'd do it just to piss me off, even if he needed the parts. So before handing over the package, I produced the sandwiches.

'Peace offering.'

'What's this? The plastic container I gave him looked kid-sized in his hands.

'Sandwiches. Roast beef, mustard, lettuce and tomato.'

'Well, you've saved me Scarface. Roast beef? My favourite. Leave that package ... Pass me your scanner. I'll sign for you.'

11

Conflicts when out delivering mail seemed inevitable from my admittedly subjective viewpoint. You had to put up with them to earn your money. But it was more annoying when bitterness and pettiness entered my place of abode. A stranger had started shouting in the lounge, 'Where are my fucking dogs!?'

'They ran away,' I heard Rachel scream.

She sounded terrified. Great, a disturbance when I'd finally found something good to watch on YouTube. What was going on?

I got off my laptop and ran out to the lounge. 'Hey now, calm down,' I said to the scruffy, but reassuringly small man right up in Rachel's face.

'Fuck off' he yelled turning my way. 'This is none of your business.'

There was alcohol on his breath and another smell hit me after the booze, a mouldy one: the smell of clothes that had been put away damp. He had a scraggly beard, a tea-cosy hat, and held two medium-sized dogs on leashes.

They started barking madly at me, but in my expert post-man's opinion they didn't look like biters. I had met this character before, but it took a moment to place him.

'I live here, it's my business,' I said. 'Why don't you take it easy?'

'You're a bloody renter. She's the one with the lease. Go on, fuck off back to your room.'

He didn't remember me. The last time I'd seen him he suggested solar panels for my Kurrus and then I crashed my trailer. He'd been wearing that same tea-cosy hat.

'I'm not going anywhere.'

'You'll fuck off if you know what's good for you, Tictac. I want the police here because she's stolen my dogs. The police always come when there's a woman in distress.'

'I see, but you should stop abusing people and wait outside.' What a rude individual, I thought.

Meanwhile, Rachel had called 111 and was talking with the operator. 'His name is Robert. He's wearing a beanie and a chequered shirt. He's got missing teeth and a pot-belly, he's around five foot eight.'

'I'm five ten!'

'Come on man. You can stay here, but you should wait outside. Otherwise, you're trespassing,' I said to Robert, taking on the role of the calm negotiator.

'Fuck you!' He glared at me.

I guessed he wanted to turn violent but couldn't will himself to do so. I stared at him, waiting.

'OK, Tictac I'll wait by the door.' He had to give the dogs a good tug to get them outside.

Once I'd convinced him to stand outside, I knew I'd won. I stood in the doorway watching him.

He shuffled his feet. 'I'd like to smash you, but I'd get in trouble ...'

I didn't answer. He didn't mean it. He looked me up and down, pausing at my skinny ankles, making me self-conscious. Next confrontation I'd need to put on long pants. I looked at his face carefully, trying to figure out if he was insane.

'What are you gawking at, Tictac? You're a Neanderthal to believe her. Rachel's a liar, she stole my dogs. Go on, ask her. I know you won't. Typical.'

Again, I didn't answer. He fell silent for a minute.

'Do you have a car here?'

'None of your fucking business! I'm not leaving. I want my dogs.' His assertiveness now relied entirely on the f-word.

'But I don't get it, you've already got dogs.'

'Not these ones, numbnuts. My puppies are the ones Rachel stole.'

'I can see you have a grievance, but this is not the way to go about it.'

'Yes, it is. I went to talk to the police, and they didn't listen. But they'll come now. I've been talking to pig hunters, and they said the dogs wouldn't have run away.'

I couldn't fathom where the pig hunters fitted in. This was his plan? Make a stink to get the police around. Lord Almighty, what an idiotic attention seeker.

At this stage, a new voice entered the fray. 'Hey, why don't you fucking leave!' The next-door neighbour had appeared on his front porch. Wearing a Judas Priest T-shirt, he had an even bigger pot belly than Robert.

'You fuck off, you Neanderthal, go back inside, Tictac,' Robert attacked. 'Why don't you get a job in a bakery, dough face.'

I thought I was Tictac? I was miffed as I realised Robert rehearsed his insults and didn't pick them for a specific person. Disappointing.

As the shouting between these two kicked off, the dogs started barking again. Our neighbour was trying to help but I'd had enough of all the noise.

'Alright,' I said, 'I'm closing the door now. Try and stop me and it will be assault.' I reached for the doorknob, but Robert grabbed it first.

'Touch me and it'll be assault too,' he said.

'No, it won't, because you shouldn't be here.' I wasn't sure of the various legal ins and outs, but neither was he. I saw defeat in his eyes.

'Oh. okay.' Robert let go of the door handle and turned around. Tails between their legs, he and his dogs made their way off the property. I glanced across at the adjacent porch in time to see the neighbour pull the fingers at the retreating Robert.

Rachel had locked herself in the bathroom and now emerged. I hoped Robert had driven off to prepare insults to use on another day. But when the two policewomen arrived, they said they had talked to him, and he was sitting in his car at the top of the driveway.

'You gonna let him stay there?'

'He's well known to us. All talk, that guy. No real threat.'

Benign until proven malignant, then. Didn't they notice he stunk of booze and think of breathalysing him? As a positive, the police officers were the best-looking women

I'd seen all week. The taller one had blond hair, high cheekbones, and stylish earrings. The shorter one had curves and couldn't have been older than twenty-three. I hoped they knew kung fu.

'What's wrong with him?' I asked.

'Oh, I couldn't tell you what is wrong with him medically,' the shorter one answered. For me, this was a good Kiwi answer: no arbitrary speculation. Keep it practical. I reckon we are the least metaphysical people on Earth. Well, I don't think that's true for Māori, but it is for Pākehā. Rachel told the police she'd been looking after some puppies for Robert, and they'd run away when she was walking them. This was a lie, and the officers knew it. Not that it mattered. They needed her details before taking off.

'What's your occupation, Rachel?'

'None, at the moment, I'm on a benefit.'

The way she answered, the shame in her voice ... heartbreaking. Next question: date of birth. She was pushing sixty.

Later I got the essentials of the story out of Rachel. Robert begged on the street downtown. Rachel had wanted to help him. She befriended him and eventually invited him to dinner at the flat. So, he knew where she lived. Had there been some romance between them? Surely not. Anyway, things had gone sour. She hadn't been able to stand the way he treated his dogs. He couldn't stand women. When he had got hold of some puppies, she had offered to look after them for a spell. Then she'd skipped town for a while and found the puppies new homes. Now he wanted them back and wasn't going to give up. Dogs were everything to him. Sure, he didn't take them to the vet. Sure, he begged for money to buy dog food and then spent it on booze. But I wondered if she'd made the right call to take those puppies away from him? As he said, they were his dogs.

Rachel worried Robert would be back. I knew he wouldn't. He'd wake up somewhere hungover and unhappy, if not contrite. At least he still had two dogs. And what about her? She said she'd never help a homeless person again. She'd wanted to help him in the beginning, but her soft heart for dogs had got in the way. I didn't have the empathetic ability to penetrate the world of pain of being in your late fifties and on a benefit. I'd helped her in a small way by seeing off Robert. That was as benevolent as I got.

In the meantime, I needed to get some sleep before tackling the following day's mail.

12

The next morning, I accepted a new problem at the depot with the utmost grumpiness. The sorting machines at HQ were refusing to count standard-sized envelopes. I pictured the bearded ginger I'd met on my training trip appearing from behind a massive sorting machine, spanner in hand, 'Fucking Chinese programmed them to stop counting mail after a certain number of years. Communist sabotage.'

The machines were made in Japan, but you shouldn't correct your imagination. As a result of this malfunction, we had to do manual counts of thousands of letters. Johnno enjoyed messing with me:

'32, 33, 34, 35, 36, 37,' I mumbled, finding it helpful to count out loud.

'Hey, listen to this, 35, 36, 34, 35, 32, 43, 52, 49 ...'

'You bastard, Johnno. I've lost my place!'

'Ha, ha, that's the point, mate!'

A storm had been battering many parts of the North Island and a long, wet day awaited us. But then it got better: Mavis called an impromptu meeting.

'I'll wrap this up in a minute,' she began, but looking at her face I knew she'd talk for ages. Today she was 'up' or energised Mavis with red cheeks of broken capillaries and the voice of an angry seagull. 'Down' Mavis had mauve bags under her eyes and a gravelly croak.

'I need to talk about your scanning of parcels,' she squawked. 'It's important. The customer is driving this, not us. They want accountability if something goes missing.'

I restrained a groan. Driven by the customer, I'd heard that one before. The customer would want their parcels teleported to their door next. I was starting to agree with the Luddites about the damage the constant demand for new technology-facilitated conveniences caused. Then I remembered the hassle of counting all those letters and I changed my tune: technological convenience was great—if the machines actually worked.

'You lot have gotta scan to protect yourself,' Mavis continued. 'If a package is missing and we have no proof of delivery scan, we might have an official meeting with you about where it is. If you didn't scan in the right place or didn't scan at all and it hasn't been delivered—well, where is it? Have you still got it? I'm not talking about anybody here now, but people can't help themselves from ripping the company off. Two years ago, we had to fire a guy for stealing a packet of chippies from the vending machine. Theft is a serious issue. I know it's raining, and I want to wrap things up so you guys can get on the road, but I've got to mention something else. People have been spilling coffee around the place. And I wonder, would you guys do this in your own homes? Drip coffee all over the place. I mean at your mum's place. No, you wouldn't. If you're having a hot drink outside the smoko room, you must have a lidded cup. It's a rule, okay, and that doesn't mean putting your hand over the cup. I think of this place as my home and so should you. And no hot drinks on the sorting floor, of course.'

You should treat it as your home. This was classic admonishing, the stuff we'd all had in primary school. No doubt enjoying herself, Mavis wanted more:

'Almost done, but one more thing. Smokers are taking chairs outside and never bringing them in.'

Back at our sorting cases, nobody spoke. Everyone was incensed by the long meeting on a rainy day and the insinuation that if you missed a scan, you might have stolen a parcel. The radio remained off. The only sound was the clack of letters getting slotted. This was a moment for Ross to speak up, but he'd called in sick—so much for the immune-boosting properties of raw garlic.

On the case next to me Johnno whispered, 'Don't worry mate—this trouble won't last long. The new generation of scanners will protect us from making mistakes, they'll alert you if you're scanning in front of the wrong house. They are already using scanners like this in ...'

'Let me guess, Singapore.'

'No, Luxembourg.'

Great, another fool who believed technology was here to make our lives easier. Old school Johnno should've known better.

At break time, Johnno gave me the lowdown on the guy fired for stealing a packet of chips.

'He's in maximum security now, mate. The chippie thief. Before your time, but Mavis still loves bringing that story up.'

'What happened?'

Johnno, still exasperated by the incident despite the time which had elapsed, put his hand to his hairline and shut his eyes.

'A packet of chippies fell down in the vending machine and the offender, a fat bastard, put his hand through the flap to take them. He didn't rock the machine or violate it with a straightened-out wire coat hanger or anything like that. But for Mavis, and those above her, a crime had been committed. Technically I suppose it had, but we all know if you can get something free from a vending machine you must do it.'

'What do you think about Mavis demanding no scanning mistakes?' I asked. 'Where is the incentive for us? Asking for more and offering nothing. That's how the company acts ... no doubt charging more than they used to for their world-class service.'

'Steady on, you sound like your mate Ross. The incentive of scanning properly is you don't get into trouble, ha ha.'

'I wish Ross had been here during that brief. I bet he'd have said something to Mavis.'

'Has he said anything to her in any of the other meetings? No. He just lets his anger stew and one day he'll do something stupid. Truth is, Ed, I think your mate is a dickhead. And not only that, a psycho too. He reminds me of that bloke who killed people in the States ...'

'The Unabomber.'

Nah, the Unabomber was smart. He didn't get caught for years. Your mate Ross will last five minutes here, mark my words. I'm thinking of Joseph M. Wright.'

'Who was he?'

'I thought you had a history degree, brainbox?'

'Cheap shot, mate. I can't know everything.'

'Fair enough. Well, I like my American true crime. Wright killed four people including his boss. A famous going postal case. Your mate Ross is a candidate for doing something similar.'

'In an alternative universe where he works for the US Postal Service?'

Finished with his marmite sandwich, Johnno stood up and looked at me with his I-don't-get-enough-sleep eyes. 'Some postie's going to go loony here in this country one day, mate. I'd love to say I picked it before it happened. The local paper might interview me about the case.'

'Yeah, that'd be great. Make you feel good.'

I regretted saying that for a second, but Johnno smirked in appreciation of my sarcasm.

'Have a good day out there. Rain seems to have eased off a bit, eh?

'Yeah, you have a good one too, Johnno.'

13

Rachel was watching a comedy in the lounge. Her cackle burst through my thin bedroom door. I searched for my earbuds but couldn't find them. My afternoon nap would have to wait until she turned the telly off. At a loss for what to do, I remembered my conversation with Johnno. I wanted to investigate the mass murderer he'd told me about named Wright. Johnno had joked Ross was like Wright. Could there be something in that? I got googling and soon found articles about the case in the *Boston Gazette* database. Joseph M. Wright grew up in Boston and studied biology for many years before becoming a mail carrier. His PhD thesis focused on sea snail reproduction. Unable to find an academic position, he accepted a role at the United States Postal Service to repay his sizeable student loans. He then got stuck in the job. A killer mailman with a doctorate was an anomaly but his stockpiling of weapons followed the bog-standard mass-shooter playbook. Wright—he insisted people call him Dr Wright—went to work one morning and went postal, as the *Boston Gazette* reported.

Dr Wright emerged from a basement locker room at the post office building in Brockton, Massachusetts, and surrendered to members of the Plymouth County SWAT team at 8 am. He had shot dead three of his colleagues. Wearing a Vietnam War era military uniform that had belonged to an uncle, he carried a 9mm Beretta, an antique Sten gun, a Kris-style dagger, and four grenades.

Despite plans to go out in a blaze of glory, Wright surrendered after about twenty minutes of negotiating.

The four USPS employees shot at the mail depot were not his only victims. The night before, Dr Wright had broken into his supervisor Caroline Robinson's apartment and stabbed her to death. Wright was allegedly angry with her for taking him off a mail route that he had been doing for ten years.

A postie with academic qualifications who hated their supervisor. A tale of woe too close to the bone for me. However, I didn't see anything in Wright that reminded me of Ross. Next, I googled 'going postal.' The simplest definition was: 'Becoming angry enough to go on a murderous rage.' The phrase was coined after a spate of shootings involving United States Postal Service employees in the 90s. However, a study in the early 2000s showed that murder rates at USPS workplaces were lower than in other industries in the USA. Probably the next major study would prove the opposite.

I stopped myself there; continuing to investigate mass shootings by US postal workers would get me down. Turning my internet investigations closer to home, in New

Zealand the most lurid stories of criminal posties involved the hoarding of mail. A rural delivery driver held the record for most items undelivered. People noticed but Post wouldn't investigate him until one determined resident prepared a list of complaint numbers from the delivery route. To do this, she went around the area knocking on doors, asking if others had any lost mail, and if so, had they opened an investigation with Post. 'Please give me the case number,' she'd say. This resident must have been a right old busybody. The real victims of the hoarding were the posties who had to urgently deliver the 15,000 items found in the offender's garage.

Rachel continued to cackle away at the TV. She could keep at it for hours. I lay in bed and tried to relax and remember where things had gone wrong; when had I lost the ambition to have a career? Well, right at the beginning. At school, I'd had vague thoughts of becoming a lawyer. In my final year of secondary school, I opted to join a group visiting a law firm for work experience day. A woman of twenty-five showed us around the law offices. Her downtrodden air contrasted with her smart clothes and good figure. She gave a summary of the work and long hours. The best thing about working there, she said, was morning teatime when they wheeled a cart around to your cubicle with different cakes and muffins on it. I assumed you had to pay for them. She did a poor job explaining what it was like to be a lawyer. Doubtless, it had more rewards than met the eye, but I was too young to figure that out. I got the idea she lived for morning tea only. Terrible. I gave up on wanting to study law. For a while, I gave up on studying full stop. Then I started again because studying helped me pass the hours at school.

My school was situated in an upmarket neighbourhood but to prove the toughness of the environment they mandated that the boys—there were only boys—wear shorts in winter. We had long woollen socks that had to be pulled up. Places at the school were sought after so they let too many kids enrol there. Between classes, crowds formed in the hallways, giving the younger boys a chance to crush each other against the walls of the maths or English department while lining up outside classrooms. Great fun. A favourite method of bullying was to turn someone upside down and loop their belt over one of the metal poles adjacent to the taps used to clean muddy rugby boots. Turning the taps on full bore, the victim had no chance to get away before being thoroughly soaked. I could go on and on about the boys' boarding school style antics that happened. For the first year it was amusing, the next four years it bored the hell out of me.

After visiting the law firm in the morning, we had the rest of the day off. Still in my uniform, long socks and all, I walked over to the university campus a few blocks away. It was breaktime between lectures, and there were girls everywhere. Now as a postman over thirty, I found it hard to imagine a time when uni girls were older than me. I had a revelation on that walk—school wasn't forever—hope existed. I wasn't sure how, but the sexual frustration would one day be over. No lurid images were in my mind then—the girls looked pretty walking around under the arching elm trees, that's it. Probably the most pornographic things I'd seen at that stage were *Playboy Magazine* and *Basic Instinct*. A sheltered teenager.

Walking through the campus did me good. It lifted my spirits after encountering the woman at the law firm who lived for morning tea. She was right though; morning tea is the greatest thing in the world of work. At the post office, we didn't have a fancy trolley with cakes and muffins. Our options were the vending machine, tucker truck, or what you brought in yourself. Most of us were happy with that—and don't forget the monthly shouts.

14

I swung into the depot at three. I would've made it by two-thirty if I'd worked to my potential, but I didn't have the dopamine supply to be motivated every day. In the interchange, I saw Dawn scribbling on her docket. I knew she'd be recording the details of her day down to the last detail. Process 6:59, bog break 9:52, process II 9:56, pull down 10:38, smoko break 11:00, loading 11:15, travel 11:27, delivery 11:43, finish 2:54. She pursed her thin lips in concentration. I noticed her new haircut—a style called sensible. Her dye job had been updated too, an even brighter red.

She looked up from her docket and frowned at me. 'You've finished at last, have you?'

'Yeah, Mavis gave me some extra. You?'

'Did almost two runs.'

So proud of herself. She needed taking down a peg. 'Still, you do that a lot and I haven't seen you here this late before.'

'Trying to be smart, are we?'

A large truck now entered the interchange. The driver, all moustache and thick neck, got out, walked over to the forklift and was soon hurtling around, loading cages onto the truck. Those cages would return before sunrise the next day full of courier parcels for us to deliver. The forklift belched more black smoke than it should have. Dawn and I got out of the vicinity quickly.

While we were getting our bags out of the lockers, Dawn glimpsed my supply of canned tuna.

'You make me sick eating that stuff straight from the can—what are you, a bloody cat?'

'You're afraid of cats, right?'

'Shut up.'

Dawn didn't like eccentricities in others. My eating tuna from the can, Ross's garlic sandwiches, and Johnno's unexplained hatred for the Tucker-Truck Lady appalled her. However, when it came to her own beliefs about the job, she was a contrary sort. On a mundane level, this meant she liked delivering in areas everybody else hated. That was fine, she could take them. Of greater amusement, she insisted cats were more dangerous than dogs. A few years back, a cat had run out in front of her bike and forced a swerve. She had crashed into a tree and got knocked out. In the statistics, cat-caused accidents sat behind magpie and hedgehog incidents in terms of frequency.

'Not true! People just don't report them,' Dawn told us.

'Right, I'd be too ashamed!' Johnno countered.

Dawn's contrary side gave me a few laughs. I thought of her as a Heyoka or sacred clown. In some Native American cultures, Heyoka played the social role of someone who always did the opposite of accepted practice. In a documentary on YouTube I'd watched, Heyoka bathed themselves in the dust and threw buffalo shit into teepees and yelled, 'Food!' This behaviour helped people question the norms of society and avoid mindless social conditioning. Using a cultural reference closer to home to describe Dawn might have been nice—something from Māori culture. But choosing something distant from your environment lessens the risk of somebody misinterpreting your intentions and getting offended.

The team generally appreciated Dawn in her Heyoka role because she'd gladly do unpopular runs with long driveways and hills. However, when it came to the Kurrus, her contrariness played right into the company's hands. Most of the team agreed the Kurrus sucked but Dawn liked them. Word was the company had already made a deal with Kurrus in Switzerland and purchased a fleet for the entire country. A few months after the trial at our depot began, Post HQ had announced that the Kurrus would be rolled out in Auckland. Dawn had flown up there to give a talk. I joked that she was being paid by the Swiss to give the vehicle a good rap. I also asked her when her statue was going up in Zurich. She didn't get that though. Some of the other posties weren't so lighthearted in their appraisal of her.

'Bloody woman would ride a horse backwards,' Johnno said. 'She's a nutter. A psycho. Haven't seen her husband lately? Maybe he's rotting in their caravan? Have you delivered mail to her house, Ed?'

'No, I haven't had the pleasure.'

'Sounds like she's got ten German shepherds in the backyard from all the barking. No postie's ever been stupid enough to go in and check. Why do they have so many dogs? Something weird her husband's got going on there. Maybe he's cooking up P and the dogs are security? I dunno.'

The fact that Johnno had also recognised her contrariness pleased me, but I didn't like him calling her a psycho. He thought Ross was a psycho too. Didn't he know the only psycho around the depot was Mavis?

Dawn got a hard time from Joyce about her trip to Auckland, 'What are you going to tell them about those Kurrus? That spending twenty grand a piece, they still couldn't find something to protect us from the rain? They'll love that. It rains every day in Auckland. And imagine trying to drive those things in Auckland traffic!'

Joyce thought living in Auckland was on par with Baghdad circa 2004. I'd noticed this was a common attitude towards our nation's Big Smoke for someone like her who'd grown up rurally.

Dawn, the brave warrior, made a defiant statement to Joyce and her critics in the smoko room:

'You guys might not like that I got a free trip to Auckland and people want to listen to what I say, but at least I've got some get up and go. You lot remind me of a computer game I play called Sniper. The main character sneaks around looking for the target, he can climb up walls and use all kinds of weapons. The target can hide and shoot back. Then there are the bystanders wandering around. They run away if you show your weapon and bleed if you shoot them. They don't have enough programming to do anything else. That's you guys, shadows, NPCs, nonplayer characters in a video game. Irrelevant and negative, too.

The company is going for the Kurrus, why not embrace them?'

I found it endearing that she played shoot-em-up games. This was several years before calling people NPCs became a popular insult on alt-right forums, so Dawn's use of the term was new to me.

Complicated programming wasn't necessary for the interactions in the game I was stuck in. The people I encountered when out on delivery stuck religiously to the following:

'More bills, eh?'

'Got some bills for us, have you?'

'Don't want no bills!'

'Good day for it.'

'Least it's not raining.'

'Oh, good timing.'

Worse still, I couldn't break my programming in my replies.

'Yep.'

'Have a good one.'

'Catch you later.'

15

Not having much mail, I decided to take my second fifteen-minute break early. I turned off my Kurrus and climbed a small hill. A great spot to take a breather. In the park below me, pōhutukawa trees lined an expanse of grass where a man walked his bearded schnauzer. A woman entered the park with what looked like a skinny Labrador. A cross of some sort. Both dogs were off their leashes.

I never tired of observing this kind of human communication via canine. The lab-cross raced across the well-mown grass. The schnauzer spotted its approach late. Nervous at seeing such a big creature bearing down, he managed to collect himself for the salutations and gave the lab's face a perfunctory sniff while wagging his short tail. The lab, dead keen to play, circled, sniffed, and jumped in and out of range. The woman, getting frantic, called for her dog to come back, mortified by its disobedience. The man's body language conveyed a suitable amount of annoyance. The lab, giving up on the schnauzer, raced back to its owner. The dogs had penetrated and intermingled the energy fields of the two people. Now, both parties went their opposite ways. The lab rushed onto a big pile of dirt, the best thing in the world. The schnauzer got back to his meditative trot. The man and the woman worked on forgetting their awkward almost-inter-action. If their refusal to talk to each other looked like grumpiness and some kind of character fault, you could be sure they made up for this by how well they treated their dogs. I reckon if you give most people a pet dog, the positive aspects of their humanity will come out. I'm sure even Robert the homeless house invader was nice to his dogs.

When I started delivering again after my break, I didn't have the knot in my stomach that the apprehension of chance encounters with the public usually caused. Re-membering the public nearly all had pet cats and dogs they loved made them seem less monstrous.

On the front door of a single-storey house that needed a lick of paint, a note on an A4 piece of paper taped to the door said:

'Dear Postie, please bring package to me in lounge at the end of corridor. Can't move. Broke my foot,'

Down the corridor, with a heavy box in hand, I passed a scene of slaughter in the kitchen. Red sauce splattered the walls and raw sausages waited hopefully in a frying pan on the stove. The smell of weed mixed with cheap Lynx spray-on deodorant greeted me before I stepped into the lounge. A bearded man lay prone on a couch with brown upholstery slashed in several places reveal-ing yellow foam. His beanie-covered head was propped up on the arm of the couch. In this position, his double chin showed itself despite the beard. His right foot was in plaster and his eyes were shut.

I set the heavy package down on the carpet, got my scanner out, selected delivery, and beeped the stuck-on barcode. Oh great ... signature required. Meanwhile, the prone man had woken up and was not giving me the beady eye.

'Mate, open it for me would ya.'

I knew that voice.

Curious to know what was inside, I complied and tore the packaging off. Not a huge surprise, it was a box of Rusthaven Draught Beer. On the side of the box, I read:

'A traditional draught beer, Rusthaven has developed a strong relationship with "The Rusthaven Man" over the years. A real character, drawn from the heartland, The Rusthaven Man brings out the tough pride in all of us.'

What bullshit. Silly marketing copy. I didn't see the delivery of beer to those too hungover to leave the house as a great addition to our ever-expanding range of services.

'Aren't you the guy who I saw crash the trailer of a tuktuk a while back?'

'That's me. Good memory, mate.'

I took a closer look at him to confirm what I already knew. A ruddy face and a tea-cosy hat. Mr Tictac himself. Those dogs in the park had made me think of him and now here he was, the devil in the flesh.

'You invaded my flat. You remember, Robert?'

He didn't skip a beat. 'My bloody dogs. That wasn't your fault, mate.'

His eyes moved from me to the box. 'Do you want one?'

'Appreciate it, but no. Could you put your squiggle on this?'

I wanted to ask Robert how he'd got off the street and into this house, where his dogs were, and what'd happened to his leg. I also wanted to leave as quickly as possible. With him right in front of me, getting his signature for the box of beers was worth it. However, I didn't want to hand my scanner to him. Once he had possession of it, I knew he'd launch into a monologue, and it wouldn't be easy to get the scanner off him. I gave him the plastic stylus and held the scanner out so he could reach the screen. His left paw grabbed the wrist of the hand I held the scanner in. Noticing the dirt under his nails, I felt a mild nausea. With great concentration, he signed on the screen and released me.

'Can you open one of those cans for me mate? Or push the box over here. I can't move.'

I saw an opportunity.

'I'll cut you a deal. If you fill out one of these Authority to Leave forms. I'll open you up a can. Authority to Leave means next time I can leave your package in a prearranged place without getting your signature. Less hassle, mate.'

'Whatever, Tictac.'

I opened a can and handed it to him. While he guzzled like a camel back from months in the desert, I searched my pockets. I had a couple of forms, crumpled, but usable. Five minutes and another can later he filled in the form. My run ten sorting case would have a blue dot.

Blue dots on sorting cases indicated addresses that had filled out an Authority to Leave—ATL form. So, if the recipient of a parcel wasn't home to sign, a parcel could still be legitimately left. If the house had no ATL, the unsigned parcel should be taken back to the depot, and the customer needed to either pick it up or pay for re-delivery. At houses without ATLs, the postie got slowed down by writing up an attempted delivery card to put in the letterbox. So ATLs were desirable because they sped up your delivery round. But getting people to fill in the forms proved to be a hassle.

These ATLs were a new development. During the sort, you had to check which parcels had an ATL. The 'purple book' contained stickers with instructions on where to leave the packages at certain addresses—under the porch, on the porch, by the front door, the BBQ, etc. You put stickers on the relevant parcels. Then you placed blue cards in the sorting case to indicate you had a package to deliver at that address. Posties worked off piles of letters when out delivering. Coming across a blue card in a pile meant dismounting and rummaging around in the back of your vehicle for a package. A simple system in summary.

I preferred to use my memory for delivering packages. I didn't worry about ATLs—no dots, cards, or stickers for me. I didn't write cards to call. Unless the package felt like a passport or a laptop, I signed myself and left it. Some of the more process-oriented posties told me I was playing Russian roulette. 'You'll stuff up at some stage!' I only used stickers and cards when I sorted a run somebody else would deliver.

For the first month of the ATL system, I didn't bother trying to get members of the public to fill in the forms. Signing for nearly all packages myself made me fast. Mavis was thrilled, she liked fast posties. But one Monday morning while sorting I felt an oppressive presence behind me. I turned around and looked into Mavis's bloodshot eyes.

'What do we do with a signature item?' she began. 'Do we sign for it ourselves and leave it when there's no ATL? No, we don't. We've got a call through from HQ about an item on your round the customer never got. This was two bloody weeks ago. Did you deliver it or not? You signed for it according to the info on your scanner. What's happening with your ATL forms, are you giving them to customers, or putting them in letterboxes? Look at your case, no blue dots at all! I want that package found and a blue dot on your case by the end of the week, otherwise, it's an official warning for you!'

Mavis's angry voice stayed in my head all day. An hour after getting home from work, I was still thinking about that package. Then it came to me, I'd left it by the back door. I jumped in the car and headed round to the house in question. Funny when you go somewhere as a private citizen, rather than in postie uniform, suddenly a neighbourhood can seem less friendly. A shirtless, well-muscled guy opened the door. He didn't look pleased to be disturbed. The package had been for his mum, who wasn't in. Begrudgingly, he gave me her number. The mother had a more friendly tone. She had complained to customer service because tracking the parcel revealed it'd been delivered but she couldn't find it. Then—five minutes later—she found it by the back door and called back to say don't worry. However, by that stage, the complaints procedure had creaked into gear. I could see those form fillers in Wellington following through step by step, so Mavis could know about the situation two weeks later.

With the lost package mystery solved, my mind moved to the next problem. One blue dot by the end of the week. It sounded easy. I started to leave ATL forms in letterboxes, but that wouldn't get me a dot fast enough. When I came face to face with a member of the public and asked them directly, they were always in a hurry, or said something along the lines of, 'I hardly ever get bloody parcels, so it won't be worth filling the form in.' Frustrating, I felt like a novice Hare Krishna trying to sell copies of the *Bhagavad Gita* on a downtown street corner. Meanwhile, Dawn had twenty-five dots on one of her cases.

As I walked out Robert's front door, I looked at what he'd written on the ATL form. If he wasn't at home, he authorised the postie to leave the parcel ... in the lounge. What a character. Mavis picked up on this straight away when I handed the form in.

'How the hell can you leave in the lounge if he's not there?'

'Perhaps he doesn't lock his door when he goes out?'

Mavis gave me a horrible look, but I'd got my first blue dot.

16

I'd robbed her of the pleasure of issuing me an official warning, but Mavis got her pound of flesh another way. The whiteboard on the wall of the depot displayed who did which runs. Mavis told us we needed to check it daily. In practice, we'd only look on Mondays if we remembered. So, finding Joyce at my sorting case slotting letters came as a shock. She looked at me blurry-eyed and said, 'Go check the board, a little surprise for you there.'

What a little dictator. Mavis had changed things. Runs seven and ten would now dominate my life. A new run was hell for the first two weeks. You had to learn new streets and driveways. Inevitably, some letterboxes would be hard to spot. People liked to paint them green to blend in with the hedge. Let's not forget that being put on a new run turned Dr Wright into a mass murderer.

Run seven started with the long and tricky Davis Street. The entire first week, I kept missing letterboxes and had to double back. Glad to have new meat in the neighbour-hood, vicious dogs barked their heads off when they saw me. The next street, Cole Road, had houses on one side and paddocks on the other. I watched the cows over the fence to calm myself after the Dobermanns and Alsatians of Davis Street. The cows walked over to the fence, curious to have a look at me. However, you didn't want to look into their bovine eyes too long because they contained a disturbing intelligence. Next came a new development that didn't get much mail so I could gun it. Broad driveways featured Holdens, SUVs, and boats. How could they afford it? Debt up to their gills?

Number one Fairgray Place had three $60,000 cars in the driveway, but they didn't get many packages. The big internet shoppers on Fairgray lived at numbers five, seven, eight, and six. At number five, a red-eyed woman in a black singlet would open the door to robotically receive her parcel. The smell of marijuana wafted out from behind her. The big sook rottweiler at number seven licked my hand before the owner yelled at him to stop attacking me. Number eight's occupant had waxy skin. Heat emanated out when he opened the door to sign for a parcel—heat and ill health. 'Got to buy this stuff before the government stuffs everything all up,' he liked to say, 'I'm getting a deal ordering these fake Rolexes from China for five dollars a pop.' Give me a break. At number six an old lady with a creased neck slept in front of the TV. Because I wasn't signing for parcels myself since the ATL trouble, I almost had to bash the door down to wake her. Once conscious, she took an age to open the door and sign for the parcel. In addition to learning new runs, the increasing number of circulars slowed me down. Instead of getting one lot of circs a week, now we got three. We got paid twenty-four minutes extra a day to deliver around six hundred circs. On a busy day, it took way longer than twenty-four minutes because your hands got overloaded with letters. Bigger than standard letters and made of stiff plasticky paper, circs had to be jammed into most letterboxes. Who wanted them? Gym membership promotions? Those went down well in the old people's villages. City Fitness printed thousands of circulars for the same suburbs, week after week. Because of them, new 'no circulars' stickers kept popping up on letterboxes. After City Fitness, Domino's Pizza sent out the most circulars. How many times did you need their phone number and menu?

The boot of my car became the place for undelivered circs. Risky. What if someone from work wanted a lift and insisted on putting their bag in the boot Everyone had their own car of course, but I worried it could happen. On Sundays, I drove around dumping circs in different bins. Bloody hard to trace them back to me, although I could imagine Mavis driving around checking bins all over the area. I suspected others ditched their circs. If they did, they had enough brains not to talk about it at the depot. When old Joyce had her 30th-anniversary celebration, I got some insight into the truth. Joyce had the sun-wrinkled skin to prove her three decades on the job. Sitting on a plastic chair by the entrance to the depot, she'd given homespun advice to those on the nicotine train. 'What about us nonsmokers ... don't we get the benefit of your wisdom?' I once asked.

'No, you can get stuffed.'

She had a grizzled exterior, but her soft side showed itself in her kindness towards the stray cats in the depot car park. If you took your break at the right time, you could look out the window and see Joyce putting down bowls of Chef cat food. The cats allowed Joyce to pat them, meaning they'd had a home once and then been abandoned. What kind of horrible person could leave cats to their fate on the streets? Joyce generally showed me the contempt many veterans show for greenhorns in the workplace. But from her behaviour with the cats, I reckoned her to have a heart of gold. Politicians should appear with their pet cats and dogs more—it certainly couldn't do them any harm.

The morning tea in Joyce's honour turned out to be nothing special. They even burnt the sausage rolls. Unable to hold back the tears, Joyce bombed her speech. The team loved her though, and there was a good turnout for drinks Saturday night. The first time I'd hung out with the other posties outside work, it was a novelty to see them in a relaxed atmosphere. After two wines, Joyce could get her words out, 'In the old days, you did things right. You didn't deliver circs to those you knew didn't want them. And we didn't speed around to keep up with the computer. You stopped and chatted to people.'

'Come on, Joyce, don't romanticise it. We know you dump your circs, no need for excuses.'

'Well, don't you, Johnno?'

Johnno smiled. The crew exchanged knowing winks around the table. Lips moved. I strained to hear, but the clock had struck nine and the bar staff turned the music up. We migrated over to the pool table, and the conversation moved away from circulars.

I decided dumping circs in bins was too dangerous. But what was the alternative? Deliver them? No way. Then I had an idea. I'd noticed a beat-up blackened steel drum incinerator in Robert's front garden. I went to see him. The door stood open, and he still lay prone on the couch with his foot in plaster. Having come prepared, I handed him a six-pack of Tui lager which had set me back eleven bucks.

'Thank you Tictac. Do you think it's my birthday?'

'Nah, I need a favour. I want to use your incinerator.'

'What incinerator?'

'The one out front—you've never noticed, have you?'

Robert grunted, possibly in the affirmative, possibly in the negative.

'How did you get this place?' I asked.

'Government pays the rent. I was on the emergency housing list for two years. They finally came through.'

That figured.

'What happened to your foot?'

'An accident.'

That figured too. Pushing for more details wouldn't be worth it.

'So can I use it?'

'Use what?'

'The incinerator.' God, numbnuts Robert had a terrible short-term memory.

'What will you be burning?'

'Circulars.'

'What? That doesn't sound good.'

'I mean junk mail.'

'Ah, the junk! Well in that case, sure.' Robert flashed a smile of brown teeth.

Junk mail, the phrase had negative connotations for the public. Everyone was sick of that shit clogging their mailboxes instead of real correspondence. I took a note to self: say you're destroying junk mail, and people will be on your side.

Feeling good about my deal with Robert, I cranked my car stereo on the way home. I had two CDs: Queens of the Stone Age's *Rated R*, and Brian Eno's *Music for Airports*. One was too heavy and the other too light for the mood I wanted to maintain but I didn't let it worry me.

17

I found the smoko room empty. I made an instant coffee and opened a can of lemon and cracked pepper flavoured tuna. Out the window, I saw a teenage boy in a hoodie use his finger to tag on a car's dirty windscreen. The speed at which he did it indicated he was overestimating his chances of getting caught. There was nothing else to look at in the car park. I couldn't even see the stray cats. I turned my attention to the walls inside the smoko room and came across a notice that reminded me that the following Monday the CEO would visit. Something to look forward to. I expected asparagus rolls for morning tea with our great leader. Would Ross have the guts to say anything to the big boss: tell him the Kurrus sucked. My train of thought was broken as Joyce shuffled in, made herself a cup of tea, and started coughing over a sudoku puzzle. I found her smoking-induced cough disturbing. I worried she'd spit half her lung onto the floor, so I finished my tuna and left.

On the Monday of the meeting, they didn't provide a flash morning tea. We had lollies, sausage rolls, and sponge cake as usual. We put the tables of food by the wall and the seats in two rows. The CEO Alan Aitken was a large, muscular man pushing sixty. Wearing a shirt but no tie, he spoke in platitudes. Standing in front of us with the good posture of the confident, he talked about the future of postal services. A slick presentation—realistic and informed. Then there was time for questions.

'Will we be replaced by drones?' Johnno asked.

'A great question,' Aitken said, his eyes lighting up. 'The simple answer is we don't see that happening in the next decade. As you may know, Amazon is working on drone delivery as are the postal services in countries like Japan and Singapore. Potentially, it's a cost-effective, environmentally-friendly, and efficient way to deliver packages but there are hurdles. Maybe the biggest is getting permission to put hundreds of drones in the air above a city at any one time. The cost of the drones themselves would be significant. In addition, the programming to have drones go back and forth from a depot to individual addresses or various community pick-up points is proving complicated from what I've seen. The drones need to be at least semi-autonomous ... sorry, I'm taking too much time; this is a passion of mine. Did I answer your question?'

Johnno nodded. He looked impressed.

'Ok, thank you again for your question. Any others?'

'Are there any plans to increase the starting hourly rate so it's more in line with the living wage?' Joyce asked. She'd had to submit this question to Mavis before the visit. Mavis then passed the question on to Aitken's office so he could prepare. Off-the-cuff questions weren't allowed. I hadn't submitted anything and as far as I knew Ross hadn't either.

The CEO paused before answering, and I detected a hint of an inner struggle to compose himself. Odd, because he'd had this question for the last week. 'Well, we start people on twenty-one dollars an hour and the living wage is nineteen. So, I think we are doing pretty well.'

'Um, people start at seventeen.' I turned around to confirm who said this. Yes, it was Murray, the union rep. His voice had been hardly audible, perhaps indicating he didn't want to say anything. I hadn't been aware of his presence before he spoke. He must have come in late. Our eyes met briefly. He frowned, uncomfortable at having drawn attention to himself. His asymmetric goatee didn't hide his tightly pursed lips.

'Ah, well, if you'd like to discuss anything further drop us an email, Murray. I know you posties have a lot to do, so I'll let you eat your morning tea and get out there.'

And CEO Aitken walked out of the smoko room with Mavis on his heels. I didn't blame him for wanting to leave.

Murray's correction of Aitken had been weak and half-hearted. He could have jumped on that error. I hoped the CEO bollocked his personal assistant for giving him such inaccurate information about hourly wages. Or maybe he'd just forgotten what they'd told him because the topic of wages for the proles bored him. Up until that fuck-up, I was giving him a pass mark for the Q&A session. But now I was upset. The CEO made more than a million a year. I knew that. Why did he have no clue what I got? The others must have been thinking the same and fuming. For a long moment, nobody moved. I turned around again, trying to catch Ross' eye this time. I wanted him to rip into Murray over his failure to act but he sat there with a disgusted look on his face and ignored me. Wasn't he going to kick up a fuss? This was his chance. Ross wasn't popular—I was the only one who listened to him—but Murray was useless. The time was right for a new leader. However, Ross got up and walked out. The rest of the crew moved the tables and chairs back to their normal positions and got on with munching morning tea. Dawn and Johnno started talking about the percentage of missorts coming through from the night sorters. If they were angry with the CEO because of his ignorance about their wages, they knew how to hide it.

***

On Tuesday, I finished sorting in good time, pulled the ordered bundles of letters off my case, and then rolled my mail-laden trolley out to the interchange. With the fine weather forecasted to last, I looked forward to the day ahead. According to Norm's measurements, we had twelve minutes to load the mail into our Kurrus. In that time, you had to slather yourself in sunscreen and do other bits and bobs—as well as the actual loading.

'Get back in the bloody depot, Ed!' Mavis boomed from the entrance to the interchange. Angry, tired, and worried, her face was a mixture of scarlet broken capillaries and mauve eye bags.

What's going on?'

'The Kurrus have been sabotaged. Joyce has already called me. She didn't get far but Dawn isn't answering her phone. Johnno, take that mail back inside.'

Johnno didn't miss a beat. He swung his trolley around and headed back into the depot without saying a word. I followed him.

'Blimey. What's she all pissy about this time?' He asked me on the sorting floor. I didn't have time to answer before the depot door opened and then slammed shut loudly. Joyce had arrived back on foot.

'I'll kill him,' she yelled.

'What the hell's going on, Joyce?' Johnno asked, confused.

'I could have died! This is what happened ... When the light up the road turns green, I turn the throttle on the Kurrus, it lurches forward, and the front drops and smashes into the road ... sparks going everywhere as I skid forward. There's a huge SUV behind me hooting his arse off. I give him the finger and get off to investigate. My bloody front wheel is gone!'

She must be exaggerating about the sparks, I thought.

'It's those Swiss wankers: they didn't put the wheels on properly.'

No Johnno, you dozy idiot—look who didn't come to work today. Smell of garlic is gone like it was never here ... Mr Back-to-the-Bikes ... Mr Save-the-Workers ... Ed's mate tried to kill us all.'

'How?' Johnno asked.

'Go out to the depot and give your machine a safety check—then you'll see.'

Johnno and I took her advice. Sticking to the approved safety check order, I beeped the horn, checked the indicator lights, then the tyre pressure ... and I saw it. Simple, but effective. I would have slashed the tyres, but this was genius. On my Kurrus all the nuts and bolts had been removed from the wheels. Even without nuts and bolts the wheels would stay on until you braked hard or cornered sharply. I checked the other machines. Same deal: no nuts and bolts. That would have taken him hours. Did they have cameras in the interchange? Could Ross go to jail for this? I felt afraid for him. It didn't occur to me yet that his sabotage could've been the death of me. It seemed nobody had done their safety check before going out to deliver. And I'd thought my slackness in not bothering with it was unique. If you checked the tyre pressure you'd have noticed the missing nuts and bolts.

We had a few spare bolts at the depot, but not enough for all the machines. It'd be a risk to use some makeshift local bolts and an order from Switzerland would take ages to arrive. Ross had incapacitated the fleet. Success! Back to delivering mail on push bikes for now. Were my thighs up to it? The local press didn't have much to do, so posties back on bikes would get reported in the papers. Ross had made a small ripple in the universe, not so easy to do these days. I knew what he was trying to achieve but the others would see it as pointless vandalism. Ned Ludd, at least, would've been proud.

18

Sitting in the car was painful. Lactic acid filled my legs after my first day delivering on a bike. Even when I'd played rugby at school, I didn't get this kind of muscle pain until the day after. Riding up all those hills on a loaded bike was hard work.

You don't appreciate how much it rains in many regions of New Zealand unless you work outside. When it pours all day, making a dash for the office with an umbrella is not the same as delivering mail for five hours straight. Who else but the poor postie can't escape the rain? What about tradies? Builders, plumbers, etc. No, that privileged, expensive-truck-driving, class stops work if it's wet. I'd found out all about the rain on the Kurrus; now on the bicycle, I made another discovery—the realisation of how hilly my suburban mail run was.

The difficulty of riding uphill wasn't the only thing I learnt by getting practical experience on the bike. A Kurrus fully laden with mail could be driven from the depot to the start of a mail run. But with the bikes, we needed to put mail bags in our cars and drop them at strategic places around the runs for reloading. The side panniers on the bikes could only take so much mail at a time. We needed to reload three times on average to get a run done. The extra fossil fuels burnt dropping the mail bags meant the bike postie system wasn't as green as the Kurrus. Damn it, the company had been right bragging about their environmentally friendly new delivery machines.

The bikes themselves needed to be stored at a house near the start of a run if you didn't have a bike rack on your car. I didn't. Community minded retired people set space aside in their garage for this purpose. I don't know if Post paid them. If they did, it would have been chicken feed ... like the chump change petrol allowance we got for doing the bag drops. No matter how many times you reloaded, it wasn't practical for a bike postie to take a lot of courier parcels. Because of that, Post had to contract another couple of courier van drivers in our area for the time being—more petrol!

Instead of driving home to rest my aching legs, I headed for a spot on the coast about fifteen minutes' drive from the depot. Because the wind had dropped and the tide had receded, kite surfers were packing up their equipment on the beach. Where the kite surfers had reigned, seagulls now waded in mud, and oystercatchers perched on newly revealed rocky outcrops. Behind the beach and an expanse of grass, large houses boasted decks, balconies, and massive windows to soak up every ray of sun.

I spotted Ross's van a couple of metres back from the sand between two splayed pōhutukawa trees. I parked, got out of the car, and knocked on the side of the van. I could hear Ross grumbling inside. The sliding door opened, and he appeared not looking too sharp. A new gauntness combined with his square jaw made him look like a Russian gangster. His yellow polo shirt had stains on it. His socks didn't match. Wearing odd socks had not yet become fashionable. I felt bad for this man lacking the motivation to go to the laundromat. I would've offered to do some washing for him, but I hadn't even done my own. On second thoughts, do a mate's washing? No way.

'Dammit man, I was trying to sleep. How did you find me?'

He hadn't been answering texts. When I'd gone round to his flat, they told me he'd moved out Monday.

'I thought you might have left the area but figured I'd check here just in case.'

Why had he stayed? For this—to hear about the results of his handiwork.

'I'm skipping town soon. No point being around here without work.'

I guessed technically he'd quit because he'd given them no chance to fire him. A good result for Ross. Sometimes they asked you on job applications if you'd ever been dismissed and why. You could lie. A necessary lie. But those add up like any type of lie and one day you'd get caught out.

'Don't stay here too many nights. One of the residents of those big houses will report you and you'll get fined.'

Freedom campers could stay in one spot for three nights legally. They also needed a self-contained vehicle, meaning one with a chemical toilet onboard—most didn't. It wasn't a huge issue at a suburban park like this with public toilets. Local house owners tended to keep an eye on the campers. They didn't want to share their million-dollar views with the unwashed if possible.

'I'll take my chances with these rich bastards in glass houses. Go on, Ed, tell me, what're they planning to stick me with at the post office.'

'They don't want to pursue the case, lay charges I mean. They're afraid the press would turn it into a circus. Mavis and co. don't have much evidence anyway. No cameras in the interchange as far as I know. Fingerprints? You worked there—maybe you helped other people pump their tyres and put your prints on the wheels of all the vehicles. So, you're in the clear. Even so, in your shoes, I'd leave until things cool off.'

'You should've studied law, Ed.' He yawned twice. 'I'd hire you.'

'I did consider law at one stage. As for Dawn, they've offered her some kind of compensation deal and she'll be stupid enough to take it.'

'What happened to Dawn?' He asked with as much interest as a dog offered a piece of broccoli.

'She had an accident.'

'I can see you want to talk about it, Ed,' he said, accepting he couldn't go back to sleep any time soon. Wasn't he scared about what I was going to tell him? He had enough brains to guess he'd caused the accident. What he'd done could've killed somebody. He could've killed me.

'Hold on,' he disappeared back into the van and re-emerged with two pieces of grey plastic which folded out into Japanese-style stools—a classic Kmart product.

'Take a pew. I haven't got long. After my nap, I was going to study the horoscopes in the paper.'

'Why?'

'I've got a date and need a plan B if the conversation falters. It's common for people to have nothing to say to each other. That's my conclusion from reading postcards when I was at Post. I don't want to have any awkward pauses with this girl.'

'Who is she?'

'A Dutch girl. She's sleeping in that VW over there with her friend. I thought they were dykes at first.'

'How'd you meet her?'

'Hey, we've got something in common ... sleeping in the same park. An easy conversation starter. It's not often in life you get such a chance. She's an attractive girl, but not a boozer. She doesn't go to the pub. We Kiwis are hard to meet sober, even for decent-looking women. Talking to a local like me was a novelty for her. I have a horrible case of thrush now.'

'So, this is not the first date.'

'It's the first date outside of being horizontal in the back of my van. We're going to get some dinner first this time.'

'Yuck, two sweaty van dwellers mingling underarm and crotch odours. Garlic, too.'

'I'm off the garlic. Looks like you're a prude about sex. Wouldn't have picked that.' Point to Ross, and he looked satisfied about it. Time to get to the issue at hand.

'I need to talk to you about Dawn.'

'What's she complaining about now?' Had he forgotten I told him she'd had an accident? 'I've had enough of those post office people, Ed. I'm out of it now. You're fine but I don't want to hear about those other drongos again. When I walked out of the depot for the last time, I felt a wave of euphoria because I didn't have to go back. Also, I knew I'd done something for you guys ... the workers ... and stuck it to that CEO idiot.'

I wanted to tell him how delusional he sounded but I needed to concentrate on Dawn.

'Dawn is in hospital.'

I was relieved to see a flicker of worry on his face. He dropped his head, picked up a twig and started poking the ground.

'Concussion, half her face scraped off, two broken ribs, punctured lung, broken ankle. They've already operated on the ankle and put a plate in. She's okay, probably go home Friday.'

'What happened?'

'What do you bloody think?'

Again, he poked the ground with a stick waiting for the axe to drop. I watched him, making him suffer, impressed with my ability to be cruel.

'Well?'

'The back left wheel of her Kurrus flew off when she cornered down the hill on Grey Street. The vehicle keeled over, and she came down hard on her helmet and side. Her ankle got stuck in the Kurrus and snapped. The helmet took the first impact from the road but then it came off because the chin strap broke. She scraped her face along the chip seal before the vehicle came to a halt.'

'I'm sorry. I didn't want anybody to get hurt. But you're on the bikes, right?'

'Yeah, we sure are. I doubt I'll be able to get off this stool. My legs are seizing up.'

'What can I do, Ed?'

'About my legs? Nothing. I needed to remember to get rehydration tablets at the chemist.'

'No, I mean Dawn.'

So, his conscience did bug him. I was hoping for that. He should've thought more about the possibilities of his actions before taking the bolts out of the Kurrus wheels. Did the Unabomber Ted Kaczynski feel bad after one of his bombs first hurt someone? Probably not—the cause was too important to Kaczynski. But Ross was reconsidering the war after hearing about the collateral damage from the first battle. This proved him sane.

'You can go to the hospital to apologise. That's all I can think of.'

He continued poking around on the ground with the stick. I took this to mean he didn't like my suggestion. Then he pointed the stick at me and said, 'And how come you are asking me to apologise? You're being all moral and judgy suddenly. I thought you were on board with idea of getting rid of the Kurrus.'

Perhaps I was acting out of character, but I knew how to respond.

'So, you don't want to go and say sorry?'

19

After a few wrong turns inside those innumerable corridors that make up the bowels of any decent-sized hospital, we found Dawn's ward. The upbeat Filipino at the nurses' desk told us, 'Sorry but you can't see Ms Dawn straight away because there's a note on her file saying the doctor wants to talk to any visitors. Please take a seat and the doctor will be with you soon.'

Yeah right, I thought, soon like in an hour. But the doctor proved me wrong by appearing in less than ten minutes. Tall and broad-shouldered, he looked like someone you expect to be supremely confident—a man of thirty with two kids, still playing club rugby on Saturdays. But this guy had a tentative manner. He spoke so quietly that I struggled to catch everything he said. 'The blow to your friend's head—you are friends, not family, right?'

'Workmates.'

'I see. The blow has caused or reawakened some psychological trauma for her. I don't know if ACC insurance will provide cover, but I recommend she has some coun-selling.'

'Did you tell her husband about this?' I asked.

'No, I didn't.'

'But why not?'

'Because you two are her only visitors so far. She's been yelling at night. Some disturbing stuff about drugging dogs.' A wave of disgust passed over his face. 'The nurses had to give her tranquilisers.'

'OK doctor, thank you, we'll look into the counselling.' I didn't want to become responsible for dealing with Dawn's psychological problems. But it felt like I already had. The doctor gave me a solemn handshake and nodded to Ross. He seemed embarrassed. I had no idea why.

Dawn was in a room of four. Two of the patients had blue plastic curtains closed around their beds. Opposite Dawn, an old lady had her curtains open. She looked at us with unseeing eyes. But maybe her hearing was sharp. Ross and I stood awkwardly at Dawn's bedside. I couldn't bring myself to speak. Facing the wall, she finally sensed our presence and turned over.

'What's that bastard doing here? He tried to kill me. Get him out, Ed.'

I looked at Ross and gave him a nod. He turned and left the room. And then I kicked myself. I should have told him to wait outside—that's what I intended the nod to mean—but he might've taken it as his cue to escape. With Ross out of the room, fewer vertical and horizontal lines showed on Dawn's forehead—well, on the half of her forehead with skin. Fresh red scab covered one side of her face because the road had rubbed the skin off in the accident. Looking at her reminded me of a picture in a school textbook showing one side of a head and body with the skin stripped back so you could learn about muscle anatomy.

I thought about asking how she felt and if she needed anything. But it seemed like the wrong approach, so I went with:

'So, what's the update? When are you going home?'

'Home? Fuck. Friday they're telling me. Listen, Ed, you've got to help me.'

'Sure, I'll try,' I said, thinking I'd made a mistake coming here.

'It's my husband, you have to talk to him.'

'Where the hell is he? Why hasn't he been in already?' Hadn't somebody told me the husband was a nutter? Yes, most likely Johnno.

'He's ...'

She started sobbing and couldn't talk. I couldn't have imagined her crying. A traumatic thing to witness: her shedding tears decades in the making. 'Fuck, that hurts.' I bet it did. The convulsing of the diaphragm caused by sobbing had to be hell with broken ribs. The sobbing turned into a shuddering cough and then controlled shallow breathing. I got her a couple of paper towels from the dispenser above the sink and stood back as she blew an enormous amount of snot out of her nose. Instead of disgusted, I felt numb and detached. Dawn sniffed several times to compose herself. And then in a voice heavy with shame said:

'Alright, get your dodgy mate back in here, I want him to hear this too. It's unfair to put it all on you.'

I went outside and found Ross sitting opposite the nurses' desk fiddling with his phone.

'Come on, she wants to tell us something.' Without saying anything he got up and followed me in—his expression was as grim as the circumstances required. When Dawn began her story, she kept her eyes on me. Looking at Ross would've made her choke with anger, I guessed.

'Stan, my husband, has these dogs ...'

While we waited for her to continue, I stared at the grazed side of her face. As the pause continued, I feared she was going to start blubbering again. Dawn was normally an inarticulate character, perhaps by choice. Now she was summoning the energy to explain something complicated—something with painful details. She was out of practice when it came to making this kind of mental and verbal effort.

Finally, she got underway again:

'My husband Stan is like you, Ross: a weirdo and too clever for his own good. He's done fine as a house painter, but the job bores him. He's never been social and so he's had all these bloody solitary hobbies to fill his time, crap he spends hours researching. Model planes I didn't mind, his little bonsai trees creeped me out but thankfully he got sick of them. Then he wanted to show dogs. Not poodles. Too easy. Alsatians.'

'German shepherds?' I asked.

'Yes, same thing. It started with a puppy which he said had exactly the kind of face an Alsatian should have. But as it grew its back didn't elongate enough. That's the word he used: elongate.

'I went with him to one dog show only. At a massive exhibition centre. Inside, I enjoyed looking around—dogs in cages, dogs prancing about in the show area, and dogs on grooming tables. Stan brushed his dog, the one with the too-short back, and drank coffee as he waited to be called on. He practised stacking her legs to get her angulation looking good. He said her legs and hips were perfect. She was a decent specimen but flawed. She never won anything. I hoped he'd give up. He was determined though. He bred her puppies together, the ones with the longest backs. It's not unusual for breeders to do this ...'

A nurse entered the room and Dawn fell quiet. The nurse opened the curtains around the adjacent bed. I'd been worried about the woman opposite listening in on our conversation. What was wrong with me? The people behind the curtains could hear too. But I needn't have worried. The patient in the next bed was another old woman. This time asleep. The nurse struggled to get the drip out of her arm, waking her up.

'Oh, ah, oh, that hurts.'

When the nurse left, Dawn started again. She spoke fast, rambling. Ross, the vein on his forehead popping, looked like he was going to be sick perhaps because of the mixed odour of antiseptic and sickness in the ward, or from a deepening sense of guilt for putting Dawn in the hospital. I felt sick because I had an inkling about how this story about dogs would end.

'A long time after that, two years or so, Stan started winning. I was happy for him. Dog shows are competitive, and he got good at them quickly without much background knowledge or support. Hard work and research led him to success—or so he claimed. For some, losing grates worse than a bad conscience. My hubby is the sort you prefer to lose to in a game of pool at the local pub. It isn't worth beating him. He won't let you go home until he wins a game. No wonder he doesn't have any mates.

'After he had success with his dogs, he became more friendly with other dog owners at shows. I knew because they called him on the landline to discuss dog posture and grooming. Stan mainly pontifed rather than discussed ... pontif ... What's the bloody word?'

'Pontificated,' I said reluctantly because I knew Dawn would ridicule me.

'Thank you, smarty pants. Yes, Stan pontificated rather than discussed. I'd hear him talking on the telephone telling people stuff like they had to comb their dogs three times a week otherwise they'd get a matted undercoat and dreadlocks like Bob Marley. What a know-it-all! But good for him because as I said he's not the most social type. I saw these calls as a positive development.

'Then one puppy came along that Stan said would win everything. He had the great face of his grandmother and the long back of his parents. His back was so long, almost deformed—that was the standard for the breed. But this dog hated judges and attacked them ... even drawing blood. Luckily the judges loved dogs otherwise Stan's darling might have been put to sleep. A dog with a bad attitude and he wasn't the only one. Stan's dogs had become so purebred ... inbred ... they had temperament problems.

'He started giving them something to calm them down. For the pretty one, Stan came across a successful formula of painkillers for his long back and something to stop him from panicking and biting judges. The mutt did bloody fantastic after that! Best in breed, best in show.

'The next generation was lethargic due to inbreeding. Christ, they'd sleep twenty-three hours a day if left alone. They didn't live in the house. Stan built kennels for them out the back. I avoided them if I could. The judges couldn't check the posture of a sleeping dog. That's where the amphetamines came in. Stan started slowly with small doses to pep them up when needed. He didn't start going down the road to the neighbourhood bowling club because he wanted to play bowls, boys. He'd found a dealer there. Can you believe that! Someone sold amphetamines to those geriatric lawn bowls players. For a time, the amphetamines worked great. But soon the dogs started howling for their fix. That's when I cottoned on that something was wrong.

'The dogs wanted drugs more and more often and so the barking and howling got worse. The neighbours complained. Last Saturday, I confronted Stan. He wouldn't tell me the truth, so it came to blows. He's not a big man and I've been violent with him before. I'm not proud of it. It sounds like a cliché of the dragon wife, but I got the wooden chopping board and started bashing him with it. Then he gave in. He could take the pain of being hit—but not the shame of it. You've led an easy life, Ed, you don't know what I'm talking about. But I'm sure somebody hit you Ross and scrambled your brains long ago. Stan told me the story I've told you guys ... tranqs, painkillers, amphetamines. I wanted to hit him some more, but he took off to the bush in his truck and caravan. He does that when we fight. He went Saturday, so he doesn't know I'm here.

He doesn't take a phone with him and sometimes he's gone for over a week. Maybe this accident with the Kurrus happened for a reason. When he hears how I've suffered, he'll be able to forgive me for the dogs. He'll see me in this state and see I've received my punishment.'

Ross's face had turned grey—I felt green with nausea. What about the dogs? Had Dawn given them their fixes? I didn't think so.

'I don't get it. You haven't done anything wrong by the dogs' Ross said, wiping sweaty hands on his shorts. 'God it's hot in here.'

I was freezing. Hadn't done anything wrong? Ross couldn't see it coming.

'How are the dogs now?' I asked.

'Resting in peace in the backyard. Apart from our fight, I think the other reason Stan left is he couldn't take the barking and howling any more. He didn't tell me where the drugs were or what dose the dogs needed. Saturday afternoon they didn't shut up for a minute. The phone rang and rang. I didn't answer. After dark, I left the lights off so neighbours would think I was out. When I finally drifted off to sleep in my dreams the barking morphed into human screams. I got up on Sunday and ... silence. I went into the garden to investigate. The Alsatians lay in their kennels, following me with their eyes, tails giving a slight flicker. Some shivered, one coughed. Their batteries were empty. The neighbour stuck her head over the fence. Just what I needed. She told me her husband wanted to ring the SPCA, the police, *anybody* to complain about the dogs. She'd managed to put him off making the call for now. I told her Stan was away, the dogs were sick, and I was working on the situation. She seemed satisfied with my answer. She muttered something about the poor dogs and went back inside her house.

'Our garden backs onto land covered in thick bush and gorse. It isn't unusual for someone to shoot possums over there. I went shooting once with Stan. I missed every time, but he got one. The possum fell out of the tree stone dead. It had a baby in its pouch, red and hairless. The thing squirmed silently. Stan, ever practical, picked it up and slammed it against the ground. An instant kill. There in the garden with the wrecked dogs, it was a day for such tough mercy.

'I don't know about the accuracy of human directional hearing—whether people would know the shots came from our backyard, not the bush behind. It would have cost at least one hundred dollars a dog to have them put down at the vet. But it wasn't the money. I felt I needed to do the job myself. Like it showed more respect for the dogs. Stupid, really. Also, more obviously, I didn't want the vet asking questions. Can you take your pet dog in for euthanasia without the vet giving it a physical exam? I don't know.'

I shook my head. I was out of my depth.

'But Dawn, once you shot one, the others would've known it was coming, that's crueller than the vet,' I said.

'Dogs always know, even if you take them one by one to the vet ... I worried Stan's .22 rifle wouldn't be powerful enough, but it did the job. I took the dogs out of their kennels and tied them to the apple trees. After the first shot, I expected them to go mad, but they didn't budge. They put their heads on the ground, the way bored or depressed dogs do. Who knows the effect of withdrawal on the canine mind? The hard work was digging the holes in the dirt at the back of the garden. I worked like mad so I could get those bodies out of sight and hopefully mind.'

'How many were there?'

'Six.'

'God!'

'I know, sick isn't it. I dragged the bodies over and flung them in the separate holes I had dug. That seemed like some kind of respect, not putting them all down there together. I didn't mark the places they're buried. The only thing left to do was hose down the blood. Sunday night I didn't sleep. I was so happy to go into the depot on Monday to take my mind off things and to start to feel better, but thanks to numpty here—,' for the first time during her story she looked at Ross, 'things just got worse.'

'Aren't you scared the police will come round asking about the shots?' I asked.

'No, somebody would have to complain for the shots to be investigated, and I don't think they will. I reckon I've got away with the crime—like you Ross. Yeah, I know Post isn't going to get the police involved in your sabotage case. I dunno if you feel guilty about what you've done, Ross. What you've done to me! Fuckin' look at my face. But I'm having nightmares about shooting the dogs. Sometimes I open fire and get their blood all over me. Sometimes they keep howling no matter how many times I shoot them. What can I do, Ed?'

I tried to speak but I couldn't because my mouth was dry. I concentrated on summoning up some saliva and gave it another go:

'The doctor mentioned you've been yelling out disturbing stuff in your sleep. This is a dark story Dawn but maybe you can volunteer at an animal shelter or something, to make it up to the animal kingdom.'

'That's worth a try.'

'You're hardly the first postal worker to carry out a mass shooting.' I regretted saying this because it sounded like an attempt at humour. But Dawn was too upset with herself and Ross to take offence at something I said.

'But my crime isn't as terrible because I shot dogs, not humans, right?'

'Do you want me to answer that? In the eyes of the law, I guess so. You had a reason. They were mercy killings. I reckon you can be absolved after some good deeds.'

I didn't know what the hell else to say. Dawn looked more relaxed—the good side of her face anyway—not because of the prospect of atoning for her sins by volunteering at an animal shelter but from confessing them and having made a good fist of telling the story.

However, she wanted Ross and me to do more than hear her confession.

'You've got to go see Stan for me boys and get him to come here.'

We couldn't say no. Dawn gave us directions to his hideout.

'I'll text you about Stan.' I said nodding to Ross, who didn't need a second hint that it was time to go.

'Hang on,' Dawn said as we turned to leave. She grabbed a gardening magazine from her bedside table, rolled it up, and pointed it accusingly at Ross. 'I want to ask you something Mr Ross.'

'Go ahead,' he said in a defiant in tone.

'Was it worth it?

'Remains to be seen.'

'What the hell does that mean?'

'We don't know if they will bring the Kurrus back yet. If you stay on the bikes, then hell yes it was worth sabotaging them.'

Dawn had the magazine pointed at him like a dagger. I expected her to explode because Ross had basically said he didn't care that she'd got hurt. But her exasperation came out in a surprising way: she broke into song ...

'Three score barrels of powder below,

Poor old England to overthrow,

By God's providence he was catch'd,

With a dark lantern and burning match.'

I looked at Ross. From the look on his face, he couldn't make heads or tails of this outburst either. It was time to leave Dawn to convalesce.

'She's not having a good week, is she?' Ross said to me after we left the room. 'For a moment there I thought we were in the nuthouse not the hospital.'

'If we'd been in the nuthouse, I would've left you there, Ross.'

'Very funny. What do you think her husband is going to be like?'

'He'll be the biggest nut of the lot. We're talking about a man who gave amphetamines to dogs.'

20

A sun weak in heat but strong in brightness shone on rolling green hills. Red and white cows sat in groups or grazed alone. Smoke came from the chimneys of attractive farmhouses. Only the odd ramshackle corrugated iron shed disrupted the picturesqueness of the country we drove through. The scenery helped me forget the mission Ross and I had agreed to take on. After a while, the road began to rise steeply, and I had to pay more attention to my driving. Soon we reached an altitude where the farmland stopped, and thick bush enveloped us. I needed to turn on my headlights. The road became windy, and, as we continued to climb, an angry SUV appeared in my rear vision mirror. Typical. For five minutes it fumed in tailgating frustration before I found an opportunity to pull over and let it pass. I restrained my urge to pull the fingers. What was it about getting behind the wheel of an SUV that made people drive badly?

'Second rude bastard in an SUV today,' I said.

'What happened with the first?' Ross asked from the passenger seat.

'At a house on my delivery run, I was about to put a letter in a mailbox when a blue SUV pulled up behind me in the driveway. I stuck the letter in quickly and got out of the way. At the next delivery point, I heard someone swearing. The driver of the SUV, I assumed. So, I went back to see what had happened.

'The driver had got out of his SUV and stood on the driveway with the letter in his hand. He was screaming that it had been hanging half out of the letterbox. I shouldn't have reacted, but I told him I was trying to get out of his way, so I'd put the letter in quickly. Then he started ranting about how he'd received wet mail in the past because of me.

'I biked away but he kept at it, calling me useless, untrainable ... a fucking idiot. I turned back and shouted that next time I'd leave his mail on the ground. That put him over the edge. He was going to call my boss. He said I had no idea who he was. Yes, I knew who he was. Nobody. He walked towards me. He raised his arm and made a fist high and far from his body—not the way to throw a punch at all. I knew he wasn't going to hit me.

'He yelled out, "You fucking better be careful, get outta here, you cunt." I looked at him and decided it wasn't best to escalate. The anger on display. Wow. I wish I'd come up with something good like calling him a psycho or suggesting an anger management course. But I was so shocked. Maybe I should have stayed and stared him down?'

'None of that would have helped, Ed,' Ross said. 'Anything you did or said would've made him angrier and led to more swearing. In your shoes, I'd go around and scratch up his SUV. A guy like that has been an arsehole to a lot of people. You'll be one of many suspects. What did he look like?'

'Little guy in his forties, with a face he deserved. Wrinkled and ugly, I mean. Not a scary physical specimen. Polynesian guys over the road told me he was an idiot. I took that to be them giving me some limited support. Fuck, he made me angry. I'd like to go online and learn how to make a bomb so I can blow his vehicle to hell.'

Ross's face lit up. He liked anything to do with damaging property.

'Terrorism in New Zealand, that's it! The training camps for revolutionaries in the Ureweras first and now the postie cell. Down with the SUVs. However, petty vandalism is easier, mate—a less attention-grabbing way to get back at people.'

'Yeah, I'd love to scratch his SUV but then I'd feel guilty about it. Not a day goes by when I don't want to smash a letterbox or bust up a car. Do you regret what you did to the Kurrus?'

'Not really when I put it in perspective. Imagine what the Post CEO thinks of me. He doesn't get it. Thinks it despicable I vandalised the machines. He noticed it happened, though. How else to get a guy who earns a million plus to notice but to strike his assets?'

'The Kurrus aren't his assets.'

'He thinks they are. People like him think they're standing on a different celestial body from the rest of us.'

'You're making no sense.'

'Alright, forget CEO Aitken. Your SUV guy put bile in your bloodstream. You owe it to yourself to put some in his, in the least risky way—vandalism. You'll feel some guilt, but he deserves it. Do you think he's feeling guilty about going off at you? No, he doesn't have such emotions.'

'People who drive SUVs aren't human is what you're saying. I've known that for ages.'

Ross frowned and changed tack again.

'Being a postie is irrelevant to you right, Ed? Every day you wake up and happen to be in a situation where you deliver mail. It'd be the same for you working as a house painter or a kitchen hand. It pays the bills. That's fine, but what's beyond that?'

'This is like when my grandmother asks me what I want to do in life.'

'And I suppose you give evasive answers.'

'Sure ... We should be getting close now.' I said, happy to change the subject.

The turn-off Dawn had described wasn't on Google Maps. I had to be careful not to miss it. Ross, to his credit, looked like he had his eyes peeled. After a few more curves, he said, 'This is it ... on the right.'

Without time to second guess him, I turned onto a dirt road and my Nissan bumped along for a hundred metres until we came to a clearing. The caravan was there attached to a beaten-up grey Mitsubishi truck. Painted medium green, the caravan avoided being an eyesore but didn't quite camouflage itself into the dark bush.

We parked, got out, and approached the caravan. The vibrating cicada song boomed so hard out of the trees that

I expected the ground to tremble. From what Dawn had told us, I knew Stan would be a small man and he'd left his .22 rifle at home. Despite Ross and me being big young lads, I still sensed danger. I knocked on the caravan door. No answer.

'Maybe he's gone for a walk,' Ross said. 'Nice spot this.'

'Oh, shut up.'

'Wow, Ed, not like you to be short-tempered. I'll bang on the window. If he's out why are the curtains closed?'

'Good observation.' My gut told me we should leave.

Ross knocked with his chunky knuckles and then put his ear to the glass. 'Think I hear someone moving.'

The door opened and a short man of about fifty appeared. He had a full head of curly brown hair speckled with grey and a hooked nose. Despite being in the bush for five days already, he was cleanly shaven and looked smart in a plaid shirt and jeans. His handsomeness surprised me because Dawn wasn't a good-looking woman.

'Who are you guys? What do you want?' He looked right through us. I wasn't a people person, but I reckoned this guy might be on another level in terms of misanthropy.

'Stan, right? We work as posties with Dawn. She told us to come and see you. She's in the hospital ... had a nasty accident but she's gonna be okay.'

His face fell, either because he was concerned for Dawn, or because he realised he couldn't get rid of us easily now. He recovered quickly. 'Come in guys and tell me about it. Welcome to my castle.'

The neat interior of the caravan smelt of air freshener. Stan opened a cupboard over the sink and took out a gas burner. 'I'll make some tea.'

I wanted to tell him the basics of Dawn's accident and leave, but to refuse tea from someone we'd just met would've been rude.

'I'll open the curtains. Sorry, I was taking a nap. Sit on that bed, I'm sleeping on the other one.' Both beds had the top sheet pulled back over the top of the blanket with military precision. Stan looked far too awake. We sat in silence as he busied himself making the tea in the fussy way of an organised person. When we had our tea, Ross took the lead. 'This tastes great, Stan.'

'Mint tea with lemon. Picked and dried the mint myself. Guess you guys want to know what I'm doing out here, hanging out in a caravan alone. I'm trying to reset myself. Get some solace here in nature because I'd been doing things the wrong way in town and needed to get away. Dawn may have told you I come up here for spiritual reasons.' For someone who didn't have any context, this would've been a nonsensical ramble, but I guessed he was talking about his troubles with his dogs and Dawn.

'Um, no. Dawn never mentioned that you come up here for that. She's a very private person at work.'

'That's okay. I know she doesn't talk about me. She thinks I'm a weirdo, and my wife hates weirdos. Sorry if I'm not making much sense. Haven't talked to anyone for a few days. Tell me guys what happened to Dawn?'

So, he finally asked, I'd begun to think he didn't give two shits. Ross and I looked at each other. I gave him a nod which meant get on with it. He understood. Pursing his lips, he took the plunge. Maybe loopy Stan wouldn't care about what Ross had done anyway.

'Your wife is in hospital. It's my fault.'

'Is that right? What did you do to her, you bastard?' The way Stan's tone changed so quickly I could tell he had a temper. Ross, unruffled, plodded through the story with unnecessary details about workers' rights. But he made the facts clear: he'd sabotaged Dawn's delivery vehicle and this had led directly to an accident in which she'd suffered serious injuries.

'Sometimes someone has to get hurt fighting for the greater good.' Even I wanted to hit Ross for finishing the story this way.

Then the volcano erupted. Stan threw his mug at Ross. Hot tea flew everywhere, including into my face but the mug missed Ross. Stan launched himself off the bed he was sitting on, but Ross stood up quickly and held the little fella off with one forearm. Stan struggled to get his nails at Ross's face and body. No match for the squarely built workers' champion twenty years his junior, Stan ran out of steam and gave up. He sat back on the bed, head in hands. He'd received the first piece of bad news. I decided Dawn would have to tell him about his dogs.

'I'm sorry Stan,' Ross said.

I put my hand to my tea-splashed cheek. It stung but the liquid hadn't been hot enough to burn me. Could we leave now? No, Stan was not going to let us off that easily.

'You know, I've done something terrible too, boys.'

'Yes, you mentioned that,' I said. Did I want a confession out of Stan? I didn't think so.

'I'm up here trying to forgive myself. I've had to practise tough love. It's been so hard. I need to heal. You need to heal too. What was your name?'

'Ross.'

'Ross, you need to heal.'

Healing for Stan, healing for Ross. Good for them, but what about the poor dogs, I thought.

'I've got some special tea. I had some yesterday. It started me on the path to redemption. It'll help us ... spiritually.'

That word again—it could mean anything to this maniac. Later Ross would tell me he knew exactly what Stan was on about when he mentioned special tea. It took me longer to click.

'We'll set up these chairs outside. It's not too cold out there yet,' Stan said, handing us a fold-out chair each. 'We don't want to be drinking special tea cooped up in here together, especially with the resentment and anger I've still got towards you, Ross. But they'll be gone once we get to the other side.'

Ross and I sat outside in the clearing. The temperature dropped and Ross, only wearing a polo shirt, started to shiver. I offered him my spare red and yellow postie raincoat from the boot of my car.

'Wouldn't be seen dead in that,' he said, making me smile.

'No one to see you up here.'

'You know that's not the point.'

'The post office is dead to you, a bad memory. I get it. Ross. We should get out of here now. We've done what we said we would for Dawn. If he's in no hurry to go to the hospital, it's not our fault. What's he doing? He's taking forever to make this special tea.'

Ross lowered his voice, although they'd be no way Stan could hear us from inside the caravan over the roar of cicadas. 'He probably suspects the dogs are dead. He wanted Dawn to do it. He knows that's better than having them withdraw from amphetamines. Come on, let's stay. This is like smoking the peace pipe. This guy is all alone. No more dogs and I can't see his marriage lasting. He needs some friends.'

'You sound like Johnno. He likes talking about peace pipes.' I wasn't thinking about Johnno though, but about Robert and how Rachel had taken his dogs away ... for the good of the dogs. Stan made Robert look like pet owner of the year.

'I know, Ed, Johnno told me his Mavis is General Custer story too. Stan's dogs are better off dead. Humans can get over addiction, but animals can't. You know I admire rats, right?'

'Yes, I remember you like rats.' Now I was thinking about Johnno. He'd told his Custer story to Ross. He didn't even like Ross. I felt let down. I thought I had a special friendship with Johnno. This was like when I discovered Robert called other people Tictac.

'Well, rats have an unbelievable ability to survive and thrive but one thing they can't do is recover from addiction and it's the same for dogs, birds, donkeys, or whatever.'

'Where did you read that?'

'I don't need to read something to know something. It's common sense. People who recover from addiction have something in the future to work towards ... or are conscious that quitting the drug will lead to less pain in the long run. Animals can't figure these things out. They have here-and-now brains. Even if the humans who supplied them with the drugs help wean them off the animal will never get over the drug psychologically. They'll just stop eating and starve themselves to death if you take the drug away.'

'Not even a dog suffering heroin withdrawal would refuse food. Have you ever had a pet dog? You're nuts. So, you came up with this theory without going through any of the thousands of papers available online about rats and addiction.'

'That's right.'

This pulling of theories out of thin air was new for Ross, indicative perhaps of deteriorating mental health. At least his ideas about the evils of technological upgrades and scientific management had come from reading Marx and Frederick Taylor. I wanted to tell him about the famous rat pack study and how rats in the right environmental conditions could beat addiction. But the door of the caravan opened preventing Ross from suffering my know-it-all-ness. Stan came out and handed us steaming mugs. I've always been able to drink my coffee boiling hot, so I took a sip right away. 'Yuk.' The mint and ginger didn't mask the bitterness. Stan joined us with his mug and started to talk about how he'd refurbished and insulated his caravan. I didn't listen.

Trees blocked our view of the horizon, but I could see hints of yellow and orange in the darkening sky above—a sunset different from the pinkish ones of suburbia.

Now that the sun had gone down, Stan opened the curtains of the caravan and turned a light on inside giving us good visibility to the edge of the clearing where the trees had turned black. He came back out of the caravan and continued his monologue about the refurbishments for another twenty minutes, and then abruptly stopped and went into the caravan again. To make more tea, I guessed.

I fixated on the silhouettes of several tree branches about three metres away. The branches swayed in the wind and suddenly morphed into a werewolf opening and closing its jaws. The tea was working. I told Ross to look, but he couldn't make the creature out.

'What happens to a werewolf's fleas when it turns into a human?'

Ross considered this for thirty seconds. 'Don't know, don't care. Have you noticed the stars are breathing?'

On this, we were on the same wavelength. But where was Stan? He hadn't emerged again. Curious, we entered the caravan. He was staring into the sink. 'Look at this, boys.' A line of ants was making its way from the ceiling down into the sink. We stood watching for what seemed like hours. Three idiots saying, 'Wow, freaky dude.'

Still staring at the ants, Stan asked, 'They're dead aren't they, Ross?'

'Yes.'

Reluctantly, I took my eyes off the stream of insects. Stan was looking up into Ross's eyes.

'She killed them, didn't she?'

'Yes.'

'My dogs!' Stan shouted.

What a pathetic case, I thought.

Stan and Ross embraced. Who would have thought, from blows to mates, thanks to the tea. I heard a pulsing sound, like a stuttering pump and this confused me. I looked around trying to figure out where it was coming from. Then I clicked, the sound came from someone sob-

bing. It has to be one of those two, I told myself. Most logi-
cally Stan. I couldn't see his face though, as it was buried in
Ross's shoulder. Although the temperature in the caravan
was around twelve degrees, I began to feel hot. With the
hug between the two former combatants, I reckoned the
spiritual peak of the evening had been reached. My body
temperature continued to rise, so I went outside, took my
jacket off, and sat down in one of the canvas chairs.

21

At six o'clock, I made a half-conscious phone call to Mavis and told her I was sick. She didn't have a go at me—from the tone of my voice she knew I didn't want to be messed with. I managed to doze until seven. I opened my eyes and blinked several times, trying to clear my magic tea-induced blurred vision. Still disorientated, I felt relieved to visually confirm I was in my own room. Then I shut my eyes and, unwilling to let it slip away, I tried to replay the dream I'd just had.

I could remember only a fragment of the dream. It started with me getting out of my car to talk to a blond woman in a purple dress standing on a street corner. She smiled and appeared interested in what I said to her. I thought this too good to be true. Did she want money? Then it started to rain, and she ran for cover. The whole city took shelter, but for some reason, I had to stay outside—the fate of the postman. I thanked the gods that no dogs appeared in the dream.

I opened my eyes again and looked around my room. What a mess. One day, I'd left my washing basket outside, and it disappeared. This caused a lot of my squalor. Was it theft? Did the wind carry the basket away? I never got the answers. Now yellow and red polyester polo shirts, black thermal undershirts, MC Hammer pants, shorts, boxers, and socks littered the floor of my room. Get yourself another basket man, I had said to myself on many occasions, but I never got around to it.

Adding to the squalor, books refused to stay in tidy piles on the floor. The ones I often dipped into lived on the side of the bed I didn't sleep on.

Marx in His Own Words had been on the bed for weeks hoping for attention. I'd bought it during the phase when I took Ross's rebellious ideas seriously. It'd also helped me drop off to sleep on many an evening.

After surveying the state of my room, I looked at my phone and saw I had a missed call from Ross. I called him back.

'You alright?' He asked.

'Yeah, thanks for driving back last night.' How he'd managed to drive after the tea, I didn't know. I'd found the walk from the seat outside the caravan to my car parked ten metres away nerve-wracking. All those dark trees. All those swaying branches threatening to turn into werewolves.

'You had me worried, Ed, taking your jacket off in the cold. Refusing to put it back on … staring into the distance.'

'I felt boiling suddenly in the caravan when Stan started crying. The more noise he made, the hotter I felt.'

'Auditory tactile synaesthesia.' Ross delivered this diagnosis down the phone with the authority of a specialist.

'What?'

'Your senses got all messed up from the tea. I was fine but some people are more sensitive. Auditory tactile synaesthesia means that sounds cause you to feel touch-based sensations, such as temperature changes, pressure or pain.'

'Glad you're so up on the science on this—too bad you aren't when it comes to rats and addiction.'

'You're still on about that. I'm telling you animals can't kick addiction.' He sounded annoyed. Of all the things he could've got upset about. 'You know what Stan's problem is?' He asked, changing the subject.

'That he's a psycho who gave amphetamines to his dogs.'

'He did what he did to achieve his goal. I can understand that.'

'So, the problem?'

'That his hobby—dog breeding—was a surrogate for a real purpose in life.'

'The collateral damage of dead dogs would have been okay for a real cause like getting rid of the Kurrus?'

'Grumpy again today, Ed. Is there anything you need me to do?'

'What do you mean?'

'You're acting as my conscience. Something else for Dawn, for instance?'

'No.'

'Alright, catch you later.'

I tossed my phone across the room and laid down on my bed again. That day, I couldn't bring myself to tidy up my room. I couldn't even choose a YouTube playlist, so I streamed Animal Planet. A wildebeest fought hard to rid itself of a lion biting its neck. Nothing like life and death on the African savannah to distract one from a booming headache and mental unease. But the next program was about crocodiles in Australia. While the crocodiles looked cool, the show lacked action. Without enough distraction, I became anxious again. How could I control this tea hang-over anxiety? What could I think about to calm me down? A nice memory? I needed to go a long way back. I pictured myself as a child, sitting in my room, reading an ency-clopaedia about the Ancient World. Comforting. Nothing that'd happened to me after age thirteen bore thinking about. And the state of my room hadn't changed since I was thirteen. After a bad night's sleep, Monday morning I thanked the gods I could go in and sort mail—another day of my own company would've been unbearable.

22

A couple of weeks later, I drove around my run dropping overflow bags at specific points. Even with my windscreen wipers on double time, I could barely see the road. The mail would get sodden in seconds once I started delivering. On talkback radio, the host complained about 'useless' couriers, who 'rang and ran' before he had time to get to the front door to sign for his parcel. I reckoned he should stop doing his hair in the upstairs bathroom with earbuds in then. I parked and put on two raincoats and waterproof pants. I felt like a broke traveller wearing multiple layers to avoid having to pay for check-in luggage. With green mailbags in both hands, I made my way through the front garden of a house belonging to an old lady. A double garage stood at the side of the house and inside my bike waited for the first load of mail. I tried to not make too much noise—because sometimes the old woman would appear in the garage, ghost-like and ready to bend my ear for at least fifteen minutes.

Visibility wasn't much better on the bike, so I tor-toised forward and didn't make the third loading point until one-thirty. This bag drop was in a semi-sheltered section of a physiotherapy clinic car park. As I shoved already-soaked bundles of letters into my bike panniers, a station wagon pulled up beside me. An old guy with a full head of white hair got out with difficulty. A dodgy back or frozen hips no doubt. He spotted me and, despite the rain, stopped his slow progress to the physio's door.

'How's it going? Wet, eh! Quite the job. Keeping ya busy and off the streets though.'

Grumpy because of the downpour and the heavy mail load, I couldn't bring myself to agree with him. 'No, it's keeping me on the streets.'

He wiped his hair, now wet and dirty grey, out of his eyes. 'Keeping you out of trouble, that's what I mean.'

'Any trouble I can get into around here? I'd be keen.'

The old man frowned, then smiled and stiffly started to-wards the door. I'd scrambled his circuits, and he went into the clinic saying, 'Keepin' outta trouble, good, that's the ticket, good on ya.' At least he didn't mention the weather again. He'd wanted formulaic conversation from me, and I hadn't given it to him. I felt guilty but this soon sub-sided ... to be replaced by the frustration readily caused by delivering more mail in the rain. Doubtless, the old duffer would get the kind of by-the-numbers interaction he desired from the physio. And if the physio got as bored by that kind of thing as I did, he could console himself by thinking about how much the old man was paying him for a half-hour appointment. A hundred bucks at least.

Silence greeted me when I arrived back at the depot. The rain had slowed me down more than the others. They'd already finished and gone home. I kicked the vending machine. I'd heard that training to be a marine, if the going got too tough you could ring a bell and go home. So, if a packet of chippies fell down from my kicking the vending machine and I was caught picking them up on camera, it'd be like ringing that bell. All that happened was I hurt my big toe. I walked across the floor past the sorting cases and cubbyholes: a utilitarian scene without any aesthetic appeal. Dawn almost jumped through the roof as I entered the smoko room to retrieve the peanut butter sandwiches I'd left in the fridge.

'Geez, you move quietly,' she said.

I laughed. 'Missed my calling as a hunter or tracker, maybe. I should have a bell on me to warn people I'm coming. What are you still doing here?'

'I'm looking at the milk. Four bottles in here. We're not going to use that much. I better cancel the order for tomorrow.'

Dawn had returned to the depot a couple of days before, barely two weeks after her accident. With her ankle in a cast, she couldn't go out on the bikes, but she could sort mail and help out with tasks like buying milk.

Watching her, I could tell she wasn't the same Dawn. She'd always liked the job. She filled in her docket correctly, sorted quickly, and delivered all her circs. She had championed the company's change from bikes to the Kurrus. A model employee. She took simple pleasure in doing the same thing every day and doing it well. I could admire her for that, even if I didn't get the same enjoyment out of the job. However, now she looked broken—a shell of her former self. She hadn't been to the hair salon and her red hair had grey roots. Her facial scab had begun peeling off around the edges. She moved mechanically around the depot and avoided conversation. She sorted slowly but Mavis didn't give her the hurry up. Even our psycho team leader was wary of this woman, cold-blooded enough to shoot six members of the species known as man's best friend. Yes, the news about the dogs had got around. Everybody at the depot knew what happened. I don't know who told them. I'd been tight-lipped, and surely none of them were in contact with Ross.

'Milk going to waste? I'll take some home,' I said.

'I wish you could, but Mavis tells me I have to pour any we don't use down the sink.'

I pulled a face. Typical Mavis behaviour.

Dawn nodded. She knew how I felt.

I couldn't bring myself to ask her about Stan. He probably had some weird new hobby by now. Johnno told me they hadn't split up. I reckoned Dawn would keep delivering mail and Stan would keep painting houses for the next ten years. Then they'd sell the house and move into the caravan with a nice nest egg in the bank. Without jobs to go to, and in a cramped space, they'd get on each other's nerves more than before. Breaking up wouldn't be an option. One would have to murder the other. My pick was that Dawn would get the job done first.

'Catch you tomorrow, Dawn.'

'Yep, same thing again.'

'Keep going, don't think about it too much.'

'That's right, Ed.'

I exited the depot to find that the rain had eased. I spotted the stray cats snuggled together for warmth in the entrance of a warehouse that flanked the car park. Dawn probably fed them now Joyce had retired. I hoped so. It'd be a step on her long path to redemption.

For Joyce, Ross's sabotage had been the last straw, 'I better bloody retire, the next guy they hire could be a murderous nutter too.'

I got in my car and started eating a peanut butter sandwich.

23

Those who dared to be crook needed to call between six and six-thirty in the morning. Mavis would answer, ask about the symptoms and give her diagnosis: 'You're still breathing so get your arse in here!' Short-staffed because Ross had left, Joyce had finally retired, and for a time Dawn couldn't deliver, we had to do extra work even when nobody was sick. We didn't enjoy coming back to the depot with an empty Kurrus, only to reload and head out to deliver again. I know, we got paid for it. But somehow the algorithms didn't make picking up the additional loads worth our while. In theory, the depot should've had an on-call postie to cover sickness. Once upon a time, a guy referred to as Tattoos fulfilled this role. I'd seen him once or twice early in my tenure and admired the ink on his neck but he'd long since told Mavis to go fuck herself.

Didn't people need jobs? Didn't the post office advertise for staff? They sure did but recruiting was a process. A person couldn't just drop into the depot, say they wanted to be a postie, and you gave them a bike and bag of letters and said, 'Away you go mate, good luck.' A Recruitment Officer in Auckland handled applications. She'd ring potential candidates and ask ninety-nine questions. They put recordings of these calls through a software program to analyse the answers. The Recruitment Officer got back in touch with candidates with seventy-seven or more acceptable answers. They then needed to pass a drug test. Once it was established they weren't a pothead, Mavis called them to set up a face-to-face meeting. In the interview, she'd ask them if they were reliable and willing to work six days a week. She also gave them an easy letter-sorting test. She didn't want them to fail as it would be bloody ages until recruitment sent her another candidate. The newly minted postie would be trained up locally. They no longer sent people to HQ to get inducted by Norm. That had been a waste of money.

The newbie would then spend day one learning to drive a Kurrus. Yes, the Kurrus were back. Rubbing their hands together with glee, the Swiss had shipped an order of nuts and bolts. They must have thought it weird that nuts and bolts went missing in New Zealand. The arrival of the expensive package from Switzerland made Ross's act of sabotage dead possum roadkill in the rear vision mirror.

In three short weeks on the bike, I'd lost three kilograms. My body shape had changed, my legs thickening and waist thinning. Mentally I'd felt sharper too. It didn't take long back on the Kurrus for these benefits to reverse.

After learning the ins and outs of the Kurrus, the newbie postie spent a week with an old hand helping them to sort and deliver. An old hand meant Johnno or—incredi-

bly—me. Unfortunately, this meant somebody else needed to cover the old hand's work. Week two the newbie
started to deliver on their lonesome. We had two quitters
at this stage. The first didn't like the rain and couldn't
finish early enough to pick up the kids from school as he'd
planned. The second, a good-looking young woman, told
me she felt like an idiot in the yellow and red uniform.
She didn't like the way Mavis spoke to her either. The
woman needed a job though, so I had hoped she'd stick
around. But then she got a text on her phone, smiled,
and walked out without finishing her sorting. She'd been
offered another job.

'Damn it,' Johnno said when I told him the news in the
smoko room. 'We needed some tits and arse in this place.'

Dawn sat in the corner drinking tea. The old Dawn
would have acted offended, 'You sexist bastard,' or out-
done Johnno at being offensive, 'Nah, what we need here
is abs, buns, and crotch bulges.' But the new Dawn sat, lo-
botomised, staring at the wall. Fresh pink skin covered the
side of her face injured in the accident. Like a rejuvenating
photographic filter, this new skin lacked wrinkles.

After the dropouts, a newbie nicknamed Biceps stuck
the training out. He seemed like a long-term prospect.
Around six-foot-three, he wore a yellow and red sleeve-
less shirt no matter the weather conditions—hence the
name Biceps. I liked those shirts too, but my upper
arms couldn't take the sun like my forearms. No matter
how much sunblock I slathered on my them, they went
red. Like with the rain, I didn't appreciate the power of
the New Zealand sun until I started working outdoors.
With the ozone stripped back above, on a cloudless day

exposed skin got chargrilled in minutes. But whatever its drawbacks, suburbia with its tidy gardens, tree-lined streets, and plentiful parks looked beautiful under the sun. On those good weather days, you thanked the divine for not sentencing you to eight hours sitting in an office.

HQ thought the time was ripe for some training for the Kurrus veterans too. Norm now visited every Tuesday to give advanced one-on-one handling sessions. After delivering, I met him in the car park where he'd set up a slalom course using orange cones. I had to reverse through the cones on the Kurrus with a trailer attached. After running over a cone for the fifth time, Norm said, 'Come on mate, the others got this first or second time!'

On my tenth unsuccessful attempt to get through the course, he said, 'Fine mate, let's call it quits. We're mates so I won't fail you. I know you're more a thinker than a doer. When do you have to reverse these things out there anyway? They've got a great wheel-lock.'

I felt chuffed. I couldn't imagine Norm had ever given a break to his inferiors in the army. Clearly, he did consider me a mate. You don't want to feel flattered when someone alpha likes you but it's hard not to. That's part of their alpha-ness, the attention they give you makes you feel special.

'What's next,' I asked.

'Next? Mavis has requested I emphasise you must fucking do your safety check before getting on your Kurrus to deliver. So, we're going to practise doing the safety check. It's paperwork—more your speed, Ed.'

'Fair enough. We don't want any more accidents.'

'Good, you understand. She goes on about the safety check every time I see her. I reckon that Mavis drinks acid for breakfast, don't you? We had a few officers like her in the army. One wonders whether a trip to the gastroen-terologist could've made all the difference for their anger issues?'

I laughed at this joke—perhaps too hard. But I don't think Norm minded, he was used to people trying to please him.

24

As soon as the Kurrus returned, they started causing problems again. Their first victim was Jonno, who got an official warning from Mavis. We found out she got dirt on him by listening to a recording of a private phone call without consent. From there drama ensued, and the fallout made it into the paper:

Twelve years ago, Post was in hot water for the farcical idea that posties should record into lapel microphones the addresses of houses that could do with a fresh paint job. The information would then be passed on to painters who would target the house in a marketing campaign. Now, it turns out Post is listening to our words due to new delivery vehicles with hidden recording devices.

Think of the possibilities beyond house painting! Posties could report on the unmowedness of lawns and the disrepair of fences. Did Post, a state-owned enterprise, get these wacky profit-making ideas to try and expunge its past as an inefficient government-run organisation? Did they want to become the most rapacious of the rapacious capitalists?

This time, posties weren't in on the ruse. Post had been secretly recording all posties' conversations when driving the Kurrus. We knew the Kurrus had a forward-facing camera, but the company never mentioned an audio recorder.

Yet unaware of these developments, Johnno sounded out a get-rich-quick plan as we sorted mail. 'You start a courier company that only delivers on Sundays. Big demand for that. Work one day a week and make as much as we do now.'

'Could work,' I said. 'Here's my idea. I'm going to do a study in which I weigh the posties here every month. Hopefully, we'll get fatter and fatter because of the Kurrus. We can also compare our weights to those of posties still on bicycles. Then we can sue Post for changing the job to be more detrimental to our health.'

'Taking the piss as usual. How can you prove it was the Kurrus?'

'They'll be the only common denominator.'

'They still advertise that the job will get you fit.'

'Good point, mate. False advertising, we've got them! Let's hope they forget to change that.'

With her usual knack of putting a downer on any fun, Mavis stuck her head out of the office and yelled, 'Johnno, wanna see you, now.'

'Here we go, what is it this bloody time?' Johnno found the right slot for one last letter, then moved away from his case and towards Mavis's office like a man heading for the gallows.

When he got through his interview with vampire Mavis, Johnno told me how the conversation went:

'We heard you talking about throwing a sickie the other day, Johnno, that's no good, we can't have that.'

Mavis thought she had him but didn't reckon on Johnno's memory.

'Wait, I only told my brother about that. I called him when out on my round. How can you possibly know?'

'Um ... er ... we have a recording ... This is an official warning for you, Johnno. Don't think about throwing any more sickies.'

'What! I didn't even take the day off in the end. What do you mean you have a recording?' Johnno told me the look on Mavis's face was classic when he asked this. She'd realised her stupid mistake too late.

'We need to do something about this ... tell the union,' I said to Johnno.

'Nah mate, I'd rather not.'

I didn't say any more to him, I needed to get a move on with my sorting. Despite having a chat with Mavis, Johnno only had one more tray of letters to sort. I had three.

I'm not sure how but Murray from the union soon got wind of the recordings. And to his credit he rang the papers, and they lapped the story up. Murray pointed out to reporters the Kurrus recorded conversations posties had with members of the public at their very places of residence. Their front lawns! Quick, reach for the Privacy Act! The public had been welcoming posties to go into the nooks and cracks of their property to drop off parcels and now there had been a betrayal of trust. And what about the infringements on workers' privacy—could the union ask for compensation?

Mavis no doubt got a bollocking from her superiors in HQ for revealing the existence of the recordings. In damage control mode, she called a meeting and stood in front of us, a picture of gravitas. HQ had given her instructions on how to proceed.

'Now ... the recordings. We understand your concerns about who has access to them. None of us wants to be a target for gossip, for our private conversations to fall into the wrong hands. I get it. To protect you guys, HR has decided all recordings will be held by General Manager George. Me and other team leaders around the country will need permission from him before listening. George will only give out the recordings if there's a good reason. The audio protects the posties if there is a confrontation with a member of the public. If it's done as a workplace health and safety measure, it's legal to record.'

Nobody had ever even heard of this GM George. How could we trust this mystery man with sensitive information? The recordings had to be turned off.

Murray continued to have meetings with the bigwigs in HQ. With him threatening more stories in the newspaper and compensation claims, the company surrendered. The recording devices on the Kurrus would be turned off. Victory.

'Too bad, they could have listened to me rapping!' Biceps lamented. 'And now we won't be protected against abuse.'

I couldn't imagine anybody getting fresh with someone as scary looking as Biceps, and I didn't agree with his assessment of the situation anyway.

'Well, playing back the abuse somebody gets doesn't necessarily help. What does the audio prove exactly? That you got abused? Are sanctions going to be then imposed on this abuser? But I take your point—the union does tend to stick it to the company too much over things like this. I wished they'd get as excited about pay negotiations.'

Biceps didn't answer, he was looking over my shoulder. I turned around to find Mavis standing there. The expression on her face was rather placid. She was looking to win hearts and minds and so gave us a little pep talk.

'This recording rubbish is just a distraction, guys. Now we're back on the Kurrus and on track again and can think about the future. Things are tough in these changing times, but we'll figure it out. I know some of you are getting parcels for difficult areas at the moment but in the final solution. We'll get the courier vans to take more parcels—especially in the industrial areas where it takes time to deliver each item. We're still figuring it out. It'll all be solved in the final solution.'

Thank you, Mavis, for taking time out to reassure us that things were moving in the right direction. I hadn't been aware of the industrial zone issue. I'm sure she didn't mean to make her speech sinister by mentioning the final solution twice.

Out on delivery, I remained careful of what I said within a five-metre radius of the Kurrus.

Mavis didn't keep up her campaign to win hearts and minds for long. Soon enough she was giving me problems again. Number one thing to remember to avoid problems at work? Don't lose your cool. Name me a job in which flipping out is a good idea. Somebody rubs you up the wrong way? Tough. Manage that relationship. But it's not fair? Boohoo. Face these tests with emotional maturity. I liked to lecture myself about self-control but the Mavis of seven in the morning proved herself an expert discombobulator. She knew how to get under my skin. Because she'd threatened me with an official warning and I'd avoided it—nay, triumphed in the mission to get an Authority to Leave blue dot on my sorting case—she wanted to give me one bad. Why? Because she'd got it in her head to do it. A heat-seeking missile locked on target; she needled me about minor things.

'Ed! Your Kurrus. Where are the keys? They should be in the ignition when it's parked in the interchange.'

I went to the interchange to look for my allegedly missing keys. When I got back, Mavis was still standing by my sorting case. 'And where were they?'

'In the back door.'

'I saw that. It's not where they go. And the key tag is missing. Where is it?'

'It fell off, I suppose. It's happened before and I reattached it.'

'I don't see how one can fall off. Look!' She had another set of keys ready and pulled the tag. She made out that she was pulling hard ... a performance akin to O.J. Simpson pretending he couldn't get a glove on his hand because it was too small. 'It's on there as firm as. They don't fall off.'

If you don't know key tags can fall off, you haven't lived. The second most important thing in avoiding trouble at

work? Walk away when you feel yourself losing your cool.
I headed in the general direction of the toilets. Then I
turned around and moved back towards Mavis. A mistake.

'Do you think I stole the key tag or something?'

'No, don't be silly' she said with a little smile. This was
the reaction she'd been looking for.

Out on delivery, still fuming from my tiff with Mavis, I
took my break in a spot overlooking a wind farm. Shel-
tering from the rain under a tree, I ate two cans of tuna
and three gingernuts. Watching the lazy turning of the
windmills calmed me. This place had one of my favourite
views but because of the limited visibility, I couldn't see
the craggy hills beyond the wind farm. On a clear day,
they looked majestic and would've been a great climb.
But their lower reaches belonged to a private farm so
you couldn't access the summits. I put my earbuds in and
tried several radio stations because I hadn't downloaded
any music onto my phone and didn't want to use data
for streaming. In the breaks between advertisements, FM
radio DJs rabbited on. A song broke through now and then.
I switched to AM. On sports radio, they talked about golf.
That shouldn't be allowed. Next, I found a talkie station
and listened to an interview with a successful fashion
designer. 'Follow your dreams and anything is possible.'
What if becoming a fucking supermodel like Cindy Craw-
ford was my bliss, my passion? Could I achieve that? I
ripped out my earbuds in disgust.

I had mail in my Kurrus to keep me out until four
o'clock. Fun on a Saturday. I couldn't bear the thought. So,
this once, I decided I'd hold on to some of it. I drove my
Kurrus off course and arrived at my flat in fifteen minutes.

I shoved four bundles of letters and parcels for the second half of the run into the boot of my car. Walking to work, the sun had been shining. I'd seen the forecast and knew a deluge was coming, but still chose not to drive to work. This stank of premeditation. I could deliver this mail on Monday. Who wanted mail turned into papier mâché by the rain anyway? Sometimes you've got to be inventive to make a weekend for yourself. Back at the depot at the early hour of a quarter to one, I rushed through the process of unloading undeliverables and plugging in my Kurrus.

Monday, Mavis called me into her office and pointed at her computer screen. On it was a photo of my Kurrus with an empty disposable coffee cup on the seat.

'Is this yours?'

'I guess so. This an inquisition?'

'You can't leave your rubbish on the Kurrus. We have to look after them. And that cup doesn't have a lid on it.'

'It did.'

'I don't know that.'

'Those Kurrus are out all day in the weather, they aren't fragile. I forgot to throw that cup out.'

'Leaving your rubbish around is unacceptable. We have standards to maintain around here.'

I saw red. 'You're a bully, this is antagonistic and point-less. Why are you doing this?'

Mavis smiled, she had me. 'If you leave your cup on your Kurrus, then others will. We can't have that.'

'That wouldn't happen.'

'Yes, it would. This is an official warning to pull your head in. I'm going to write it up and put it in your cubbyhole. Remember three written warnings and you get your marching orders.'

'For the cup?' Ridiculous. I left her office seething.

Driving home that afternoon, I remembered something else important. Once something goes wrong at work the best thing is to contextualise it. Step back and think about it. If you weren't involved how insignificant would this seem? A postman in New Zealand gets goaded into re-acting by a nasty boss who then gives him a warning for a minor infraction. That kind of depersonalisation will prevent you from reaching for the alcohol. Don't worry about Mavis, I told myself, the Everywhere Spirit will get her in the end. I just needed to be patient. Happily, I'd found my Blue Öyster Cult's *Fire of Unknown Origin* CD under the driver's seat the other day. I turned it up to drown out my thoughts.

25

C orporate visitors to the depot were bad news. When these characters turned up, they projected false enthusiasm and asked inane questions. For instance, one top manager, with a super friendly manner, wanted to know if we got fuel cards for our Kurrus. Nobody could believe how much of an idiot this guy was. Fuel for electric vehicles, honestly! No doubt he got free petrol for his company-provided SUV. And when he got behind the wheel, I bet he dropped the friendly manner and tailgated whenever possible. 'High energy and confidence, not smarts, gets success,' I told the others in the smoko room. An onto-it comment I thought, but it impressed nobody.

A mundane life, seeing those same postie faces sticking letters in slots day in and day out. But boring could be good if it meant a lack of unexpected problems. Unfortunately, we had no peace from the corporate powers of progress from Wellington HQ. These right royal pains in the arse had to find something to do. Sure enough, one morning

Mavis interrupted the sort to call a team brief: a visitor from HQ wanted to tell us about the big rebranding.

Yes, People and Culture were in town. Their sacrificial goat was a young woman of the 'I just graduated from uni with an HR degree' type. Her voice wobbled at the end of every sentence showing nerves, but apart from that she kept herself under control. Johnno kept poking me as she did her spiel, wanting to know if I thought she was hot. I had adopted the habit of closing my eyes during such briefs because I found it relaxed me. I didn't want to open my eyes just to answer Johnno's question.

We'd no longer be referred to as posties, the HR Grad told us. Our new job title was IDA, or Integrated Delivery Agent. We carried courier packages and rode electric vehicles. Traditional posties, we were not.

'Being the first IDAs nationwide, you should be proud. You've done so well here adjusting to the new system. An example to the rest it can be done. Important, because Integrated Delivery will be rolled out around the nation in due course.'

Having brought along a projector, she showed us various graphs of estimated workloads on the Kurrus for the following months broken down into full-time equivalency—FTE—and part-time equivalency—PTE—hours. They had calculated these new workloads based on shorter sorting times due to an anticipated upgrade in the automated sorting technology. Too bad Ross wasn't around to hear this: another technological upgrade detrimental to the worker. They'd made us do a bunch of lowly paid overtime and now some of us would have to go part-time. Some wouldn't have a job at all.

'But don't worry,' said the HR Grad, 'voluntary redun-dancy packages will be available to those with over five years of service. And of course, we've taken into account natural attrition.'

The HR grad also gave us some good news. We had the go-ahead to ditch the uncomfortable MC Hammer padded pants they'd given us when we first got the Kurrus. The pants had been abandoned for the return to the bikes, but then reissued. Now shorts were back, and this brought a cheer from the ranks. We would be getting new shirts and jackets, too, and they would be orange and green. The HR Grad profiled the new colours as 'a striking combination setting us apart from our competitors.' Mavis had been nodding her head vigorously all through the talk but now she looked a little sick. Her normally red face turned pale green. She wasn't a fan of such a uniform change. The stupider we looked, the harder we'd be to manage.

'Like vomit,' Biceps offered, giving feedback on the new colour scheme. I had Johnno on my right poking me and Biceps on my left. I didn't look but I knew Biceps had a dumb grin on his face.

'I reckon if you have orange and green vomit, you're in big trouble,' I said, keeping my eyes shut.

'Nonsense,' Biceps scoffed, 'I've had many nights on the tiles with orange and green chuck, and look at me, I'm fine.'

'Alright, you two, we can hear you back there, shut up,' Mavis snapped.

'Now, the other thing I'm excited to tell you today,' continued HR Grad ignoring the off-colour comments, 'is that you'll each be getting a new scanner.'

Curiosity got the better of me at this stage, I opened my eyes to look at the black scanner she was holding up. Our current ones resembled cell phones from the 1980s, but this one was more like something the doctor stuck in your ear. Now I could see what HR Grad looked like. I thought about Johnno's question. It was hard to say. I couldn't see her legs, as her jacket came down to her ankles. Her face, though not unpleasant, was pastier than a Scotsman's bum.

'To stay ahead of our competition, we can't afford to stay low-tech. These new scanners are expensive, so please look after them. You'll each get a three-digit ID number to log into them, but you'll be told more about that later.'

'Who's going to be 007, then?'

'Shut up Johnno!'

We made bets on who would be the first person to drop their new scanner in a puddle. The young woman from People and Culture wisely sat down when done talking. She didn't want to face an impromptu Q&A session with the unwashed.

'Orange and green, do they think we're bloody leprechauns?' Johnno asked me after the meeting.

'I'm not wearing orange and green,' I told him, 'I've had about enough.'

'And so, we have the first case of natural attrition. Making your stand, eh! Ed is going to quit over an offended fashion sense! Brilliant!'

26

I didn't want to quit because of the orange and green uniform—I'd told Johnno that for a laugh. But resigning made sense because sooner or later Post would get rid of me in one of its restructures. I wanted to get ahead of the game. Usually, the last in the door should go first but Biceps, although a big idiot and not a great worker, got on well with Mavis. He knew her brother. They'd worked as butchers together. I tried to picture this. Biceps grinning, cleaver in hand, ready to sever the shoulder of a large carcass hanging on a steel hook. Mavis's brother scowls, cutting steaks with a very sharp knife. Afterwards, they go to the pub, a place with plastic jugs of DB Draught and beer mats that smell stale. They place bets on the horses. Biceps wins and laughs with delight. Mavis's brother loses and thinks about cutting his mate's lips off.

With money saved up, I could afford to say I'd had enough of Mavis and delivering mail in the rain. Ross had texted me from somewhere in Australia saying work was plentiful there—but another option interested me:

becoming a van courier. Contractors without direct managers, van couriers didn't get as wet as posties and earned more money. To become one, I'd need to buy a van.

On one of my rounds, I delivered to a car yard with a salesman fond of shooting the shit. A smooth character, the back and sides of his head were a constant stubble, and his goatee an artistic work of control. In an immaculate suit, the way he always had his tie loosened made him seem approachable. One day, as I handed him a couple of bills, he'd said to me:

'Mate, I'm worried about you. Don't you know nobody wants paper letters anymore? Most stuff goes straight in the bin these days.'

'Yes, I know, I'm performing a role that should already be obsolete.'

'That's the word I should have used, obsolete—you've got some intelligence mate.'

I knew these salesmen gave out compliments to ingratiate themselves to potential customers. Still, it was hard not to fall for it. I felt myself smiling when he called me smart. After a few more convos about this and that, I felt comfortable enough to ask him what I feared was a stupid question:

'How do people have enough money for these new utes and SUVs?'

'Good question. Often they lease them and that can be a great deal. Let me tell you how it works. You lease a ute for three years and after that buy it. If it's something like a Hilux the depreciation in price will be greater than what you lease it for. Let's say you pay five grand a year for leasing it. That's not much, is it? After three years, you'll pay thirty-five to own it. It was worth sixty new. See mate, it's like you get a ten grand discount.'

'Wow that's quite a lot to take in, I'm not sure I'm as intelligent as you think, mate.'

This attempt at self-effacement backfired, as he went through those details again ... and then talked about other great deals that could be had. In summary, anything was possible if you could keep making payments. And then things took an interesting turn.

'Mate, park that bloody postie tuktuk up round the back and we'll go for a drive. How do you feel about a Land Cruiser—worth 130,000? Damn thing's indestructible. Let's take it for a spin. Just for fun.'

I couldn't say no. He chucked me the key. Well, not a key but a beeper to unlock the door. Once inside the vehicle, I was at a loss for how to start the engine.

'Press this button with your foot on the brake. Geez, what year is your car mate?'

'1998.'

'Last century, Christ.'

With me in the driver's seat, we took the Land Cruiser onto the motorway and hit one-eighty. It felt like seventy, no wonder people driving big utes and SUVs had no patience with those of us in little 1.6-litre cars.

'Easy there, mate ... if we get caught at this speed both of us will lose our jobs. Now then, have a go at this stereo.'

He connected the stereo to his phone via Bluetooth.

'What do you want to listen to? Anything you like, I'll put it on Spotify.'

'Blue Öyster Cult.'

'Awesome mate, we've got a lot in common.'

It came to me that UN peacekeepers had used Land Cruisers in conflict zones like Cambodia, Somalia, and Iraq ... and that locals in those countries loved to steal them and mount machine guns on the back. I wondered if you could order an armour-plated Land Cruiser in New Zealand and how much it would cost.

We turned around and coasted back at an easy one-hundred and ten. The Land Cruiser was a beast. It had a good stereo, navigation system, and parking sensors. However, I would've struggled to say owning one would make my life better, despite it costing 125,000 more than my own car. I could see myself driving around in a Land Cruiser and everything being much the same as before. The test drive had quelled my desire for a better vehicle, rather than sparked it. This didn't make me feel morally superior, rather it panicked me that money couldn't buy pleasure or abate a sense of banality in my everyday life. Could I aspire to a boat for the Land Cruiser to tow? That at least still seemed unattainable.

Blue Öyster Cult's *Burnin' for You* came to an end, and I gritted my teeth through several grating Spotify ads. I felt like saying, 'Bloody hell, why don't you pay for premium, mate?' But I restrained myself.

'What do you want to listen to now?' The salesman asked me.

'Can.'

'Never heard of them.'

'They're a German band, very cool.'

We listened to a particularly abstract krautrock tune. Not the kind of music to request if you wanted to win friends and influence people.

'You've gone down in my estimation, mate—never mind—Blue Öyster Cult was a good call. Hey, you hungry? Let's go to the McDonald's drive-through, my shout.'

'I really should get back to delivering mail but damn, yes, I'm hungry.'

The line at the drive-through was long. I started to worry that I wouldn't get my mail done before dark. But I reasoned that I was having a novel experience and when you have a repetitive job these should be welcomed and treasured. We drove back to the car yard and ate our burgers in the Land Cruiser.

'Time's gone when going to McDonald's was a lottery in terms of whether you got a good burger or last Thursday's. Now they make them all fresh. Careful mate, don't get any sauce on the seats ... Shit!' A drop of tomato sauce had fallen onto his trousers. He scrapped it off with the nail of his right index finger.

'Mate, you got a tissue?' He asked, panicked.

'No, sorry.'

He assessed the damage—a small dark stain. 'No worries, mate, I'll sort this out later.' His ability to regain composure impressed me.

'Thanks a lot for the test drive and the food. I'd better get back on with mail delivery.'

This was the moment for his spiel:

'Mate, you should think of becoming a courier. You'd make more money and stay out of the rain. In fact, we've got some deals for postal workers. We can do you a new van for thirty-three thou that would normally be fifty. Great financing conditions.'

I told him I'd think about it and immediately his manner became a little cooler. My guess was he interpreted 'I'll think about it' as a hard no. But I really had been thinking about getting a van.

It was already three o'clock when I puttered off to finish my round in a God-forsaken suburban development called The Birds. People out there didn't know the number of the house next door to them, let alone the names of their neighbours. On the plus side, nobody ever materialised to bug me about their mail. Street names included Kestrel, Osprey, and Bluejay. No street bore the name of a native bird.

I decided not to go back to see my friend the car salesman and sound him out on the van financing conditions he could offer me. Although the money would be better as a courier and I wouldn't get soaked or yelled at, it would still be a stagnant and repetitive job. Another option was getting a job in the government. That meant writing cover letters and filling in application forms and then interviews with panels of apparatchiks asking behavioural questions:

'Tell us about a time when you had to deal with a difficult manager?' You refer to your notebook of anecdotes and remind yourself of the STAR method before answering. Situation, Task, Action, Result. Situation: an upgrade in technological capital that is detrimental to the workers. Task: come up with a way to reverse this technological upgrade. Action: sabotage. Result: reversal of the upgrade but only temporary—you can't stop the march of progress.

I'd tried to get a government job before and got nowhere—I had no idea how to answer their questions.

Well, that wasn't true. If I prepared the answers, I'd be okay, but how to make them like me enough to give the job? Maybe this time it'd be different, but it'd still take time. And I didn't want to keep delivering mail or use up my savings in the meantime.

When I gave Mavis my notice, I assured her I wasn't leaving because of the new uniform but because I needed a change. 'Bloody hell, you just got here,' she said. I wasn't sure if my resigning this quickly fitted in with the natural attrition plan HR had, but from the look in her bloodshot eyes, I didn't think she was too worried about seeing me go.

On my last day, I walked out of the depot full of joy, knowing I'd never have to go back.

'Hey Ed,' Mavis called out, interrupting my triumphant walk across the parking lot bathed in sunlight. I turned to see her spiky-hair-topped outline in the dark depot entrance. 'Don't forget to bring your uniform back tomorrow if you want to get your last pay.' Annoying as ever, but she couldn't bring my mood down this time.

27

On the Monday of my first week of freedom Norm and Mavis came to my flat. I had my earbuds in, but they knocked with such force I heard them all right. When I opened the door, I knew—yes, I'd quit, but Mavis still wanted to get me. You had to admire her persistence.

'Hey, mate, good to see you again,' said Norm with a shit-eating grin that looked genuine. 'I'm here in my capacity as head of Post security. Bet you didn't know I held that position. We keep it under wraps.' In a black shirt and beige slacks, standing next to Mavis he looked a million dollars. She wore a new work-issued orange and green polo shirt. It didn't suit her but who could pull off such an item? Her shorts exposed pasty legs marked with prominent blue veins. Despite an age difference of only five years, she looked like Norm's country bumpkin mother. He was the son who'd left home and made something of himself in the city.

'What can I help you with, guys? You've come all the way from Hastings to see me, Norm?'

'No, mate, don't worry, you're not that important. I'm here to teach the team how to use the new scanners. But we've had a tip-off you've got undelivered mail in your car. Remember I explained to you in training that we can search your car, even though you're no longer an employee?'

I didn't remember that, and I had a good memory. Norm hadn't mentioned it, but I resisted the urge to correct him. Received a tip-off? From Mavis no doubt.

'Wait a minute, I've still got a copy of my contract.'

'Wow, Mr Organised. In your filing cabinet, is it?' Norm said, his grin getting wider.

I shut the door on them and went to my room. It took me a while to find the contract in the pile of papers at the bottom of my wardrobe but indeed there was a clause saying Post could search your car up to ten days after you left the service. Hoarders weren't smart: I later learned that many got caught because of this clause. Post also wanted to search your house but had no chance of getting that condition into a labour contract. They couldn't enter your accommodation unless they found a letter in your car addressed to somebody you couldn't prove a connection with. This still seemed like a police-type level of power.

I had about twenty undelivered letters in my wardrobe. People handed me back letters they received for previous residents at their addresses. I'd put these in my pocket with the intention of taking them out when I got back to the depot. I'd then forget about the letters and find them again when checking my pockets before washing my clothes. If a letter looked like nothing important, I'd stick it in my wardrobe. No big deal—but they could prosecute me for that. Then I'd have a record. I could lie on future job applications when they asked if I had any convictions—but what if they asked for a police check? Most places did. Your whole life ruined over a few undelivered letters. Pathetic, silly ... but it could happen.

I threw the contract back in the wardrobe and went to open the door again. The two vultures were still waiting there. They stood for a moment considering my hyperventilation, Mavis with rapacious eyes, Norm with mild curiosity. I needed to say something. What?

'Pity they don't do induction in Wellington anymore, Norm. I enjoyed it and learned a lot from you.' An out of context compliment but no harm in trying to ingratiate myself.

'Yeah, mate, I remember our lunch together. You're a bright kid. You asked me some good questions about Iraq. Most trainees are as dull as dishwater.'

The tone was too matey for Mavis.

'Get on with it, Norm. He's stalling.'

'Keep your hair on, Mavis. Hand over your keys, Ed. Let's get this over with. Have you been a naughty boy?' Norm laughed. Mavis remained stony-faced. I felt sick. I hadn't done a thorough check of the car. During the three weeks on the bikes, I'd been throwing mail into the boot and back seats every day. Letters had a habit of falling into nooks and crannies.

They poked around inside my car for twenty minutes. I didn't know a car had that many potential hiding places. After handing my keys back, Norm got a clipboard out of his SUV and started filling out a form. Mavis lit a ciggie. She had the ability to have one now and then when it suited her. How annoying. She lit her fag with my lighter and then pocketed it.

'Can you give that back, please?'

'This yours? How do you know? It's a regular black Bic lighter.'

'Look on the bottom, there's a tiny picture of Batman.'

'Hey, that's cool. But you don't smoke. Why have you got a lighter in your car?'

'For burning circs.'

Mavis's fisheyes looked right through me, and I felt a prickle down my spine. Norm's smile wavered. He wanted to say something like, 'Don't be a smart arse, mate,' but restrained himself.

Norm finished filling the form in and signed it. He tore off the carbon copy and handed it to me. He turned his smile back on. 'Nothing here, mate, you're off the hook. No page five story about you hoarding mail in the local rag. Only been doing this a short time and already I've caught a couple of bad eggs. One woman had her house bursting with undelivered mail. Who could do such a thing? A person with hidden darkness in the back rooms of their psyche, I reckon. We've all got some darkness. Can't be helped, bleeding hearts say. But if you don't deliver the mail, you've gotta be punished. Otherwise, you'll move on to serious crimes. You might shoot someone: go postal, they say in the US.'

To try and outdo Norm the philosopher, Frankenstein's monster, Mavis, made a rare attempt at humour. 'I reckon this guy has been up to something. We need to do a polygraph, Norm.'

'Or put him on the rack, eh Mavis! Employ the torture techniques perfected by the French in Indochina. Ed knows I like my military history. I get it though, why people mess up sometimes. The job is overwhelming. I used to think being a postie was a slacker job. But the amount of stuff to deliver these days! Bills, circulars, and all those packages. I've observed how different types of posties work. The good, the bad, the average, and the machines. There's this woman who controls the radio at a branch depot in Palmy. She'll put it on a Christian Rock station for half an hour, and when you ask her if she's trying to convert the others, she'll say, 'Oh I didn't realise it was on that station!' She wasn't listening, didn't know what she'd tuned into. While sorting mail, nothing else gets through to her. In half an hour she can sort five trays of mail. Some people's ability to work stuns and impresses me. But it worries me, too. Why do they want to work so hard? Are they covering up, suppressing something?'

'Everybody's hiding something. Ed definitely is.' Mavis's forehead was a maze of frown lines and veins.

'I reckon he's clean, Mavis. I liked him from the moment he turned up early to my training session. He listened too. You don't know how rare that is.'

Mavis made a scoffing sound and got in the SUV.

'You have a great day, Ed.' As he said this Norm whipped an envelope out of his pocket and stuffed it into my shorts. He then shook my hand and gave me a wink.

'Catch you later, good luck with it all.'

'Thanks, Norm. It was nice working with you.'

He got into the driver's seat of the SUV. As they drove off, he gave me a wave. Mavis didn't. What ate that woman? When their vehicle was out of sight, I breathed a sigh of relief. I reached into my pocket and drew out the now much-crumpled standard-sized white envelope Norm had given me. On it a yellow sticker said 'No longer at this address' with a date from two months ago. The letter was for one James Parson. I recognised the street address—an area with lots of office buildings. I ripped the envelope open. Inside was a cheque for fourteen dollars written by a school to pay James Parson's Accountants. Fourteen dollars? Guess that's why the accountant wasn't at that address anymore, out of bloody business. You charge no less than a hundred bucks, guys, no matter how small the job. The cheque was marked non-negotiable; good. Thank God. That meant the school wouldn't be worried about its whereabouts. I went back into the house, ripped the letter into small pieces, and threw them into the bin in the kitchen. I knew the receptionist at that school well enough—a grey-haired woman who smelled of cigarettes. Must have had that job for decades, they don't hire school receptionists who smell like that anymore. What would she have thought about me ripping up the cheque? I stopped myself there and took a few deep breaths. I no longer needed to worry about undelivered mail. I was in the clear.

'Junk mail?'

I jumped so high my head nearly hit the kitchen roof.

'Sorry, didn't mean to scare you, I saw you ripping up a letter,' Rachel said. Because the curtain in the lounge had been shut, I'd figured she was out...or at least couldn't see what I was doing in the kitchen. She'd crept up behind me.

'No problem,' I said once my feet hit the ground. 'Yea ripping up a bill. They already sent it to me by email. A waste of paper. By the way, I've been meaning to talk to you. Sorry, but I'm going to move out."

She shrugged her shoulders and smiled. I guessed she took the news well because given my room's cheap rent, it'd be simple enough to find someone new.

'Oh, that's a shame. You've been an easy person to live with, Ed.'

I wouldn't have said the same about her. I wouldn't miss seeing her dirty dishes in the sink.

'What's next for you?' She asked.

'I'm headed to Australia.'

'You're a young man with things to do. I didn't expect you to stick around long.'

An interesting perspective. I'd remember the flat for Robert's silly home invasion and for Rachel's piercing cackles when she watched TV.

On my last day at the flat, Rachel gave me a farewell hug. I didn't feel comfortable with the physical contact. Her polyester jumper and tartan skirt had seen better days, but she smelled no worse than cheap soap and mothballs.

'Are you in a hurry? Would you like to see the puppies?'

'Puppies, where?' I felt excited—who doesn't enjoy meeting puppies?

'In the van.'

Painted many shades of not quite the right colour, her van was parked in the driveway. She opened the side door with a grunt and two black puppies appeared wagging stumpy tails. They whined and trembled with excitement but didn't attempt to jump out.

'Come on must be less than twenty centimetres to the ground ... you're not that small.' Rachel said, cajoling them to take a leap.

I picked one up and looked into its innocent eyes. With proportionately large paws it'd grow into a large specimen. It had a squished-in nose and already showed signs of developing a barrel chest—a boxer-staffie cross, I guessed.

'You're holding the boy. The other one is his sister.'

'You going to keep these guys in the flat? That'll take a special flatmate. Is the landlord on board?

I feared she'd tell me the dogs would live in the van.

'Oh no, they're not staying with me. I'm taking them down to Robert later. I still feel guilty for giving his dogs away. I did it with the best intentions and he shouldn't have come around here yelling about it, but with some water under the bridge we've patched things up between us.'

I should have known. So, they were friends again and these puppies had a life on the street ahead of them. I said nothing though. I didn't want to annoy her because she still hadn't refunded the bond into my bank account. And for my move to Australia, I'd need that money.

Epilogue

'How's it going?' I asked a wiry little guy sitting outside a tent reading *Harry Potter and the Philosopher's Stone*. 'Do you know where to get work around here?'

I was afraid he'd be grumpy at having his reading interrupted, but no, he was helpful. 'Yeah, cotton chipping is the go,' he said in broad Aussie. 'I've got a full gang at the moment, but Bert is always looking for people. You can sign up at the campground reception.'

'Cheers, mate, I'll do that!'

'Good luck, mate.' The Harry Potter reader's smile didn't look one hundred percent benevolent. It seemed too easy. There'd be a hitch for sure. However, I decided to sign up. I walked over to Ross's tent and called out to him. He appeared looking sleepy but agreed to go with me to the camp reception.

'Why are you so lethargic lately?' I asked. 'You should start eating garlic sandwiches again.'

He answered with an ambiguous grunt.

I'd met up with Ross in Sydney. He'd had a bar job there but managed to get fired. Then he survived on the odd shift with a labour-hire agency. Now we'd travelled to a one-hill town in the middle of New South Wales where Ross reckoned it'd be easy to find work. From the top of the one hill, the view was of orchards, vineyards, and farmland stretching towards the horizon. Ross left it to me to look for work. He stuck to sleeping or reading in his tent. No Harry Potter, though, more likely Che Guevara.

The next morning at five-thirty, sitting in a stationary van, I got my first impression of our new boss, Bert. He circled the vehicle, tapping the windows to count those inside. The way his finger hit the glass I got the impression he'd like to poke out a few eyes. A man with built-up anger. On the hour-long ride to the cotton fields, some slept while others looked apprehensive about the day ahead. Once there, Bert gave us all a tool much like a garden hoe but with a longer, narrower blade. With these, we walked up and down rows of cotton plants, chopping out weeds. When the guy at the campsite had told me cotton chipping was the go, I didn't know what that meant. Now I did, chipping meant weeding. The work was easy enough, but by ten in the morning, it was close to forty degrees, and the sweatier you got the more the flies bugged you. Bert played missed-weed-spotter following behind the team of twelve. Better do a good job when he was in your row: any weeds left behind and he'd give you a raspy foul-mouthed serve. Five feet tall and wearing a jacket under the blazing sun, Bert wasn't young, but he could take you for sure. Not perhaps helpful in his position, he wasn't one to warm to newcomers. His gang was made up mostly of harsh-looking locals who'd been seasonal labourers too long for their own good. Their expressions and body language made it clear they didn't want to be engaged in conversation. Fine by me.

Near the end of the day, we stood in line at the edge of the cotton field taking a short breather. Ross, in a sweaty yellow polo shirt, broke ranks, climbed the muddy bank behind us, and bent down to tie a shoelace. I don't know why he climbed the bank to do this.

'What are you fucking doing? I didn't call smoko,' Bert screamed at him.

'Tying my shoelace.'

'You stay in line with the rest of us, we're a team.'

'I was tying my fucking shoelaces.'

'Don't talk back to me, you bastard, I'm the ganger here. Go on, fuck off, you're finished!'

My garlic-eating buddy was out of another job. Incredible.

To top it all off, Ross had to make other arrangements to get back to the campsite, as he was no longer welcome in Bert's van. I told him I'd walk back with him, but he said no, that might annoy Bert too. 'Don't think I'm being generous, mate, who am I going to borrow money off if you don't have a job either? '

'I'm going to shit in Bert's tent,' Ross told me when he finally arrived back at the campsite that evening. He said it with a laugh, but I could see he was fuming inside. I admired his outrage. An interesting idea, shitting in the tent. It could be sweet revenge, but it was a dangerous mission. Ross didn't even know where Bert stayed. 'His van smelt bad, maybe he sleeps in it,' I suggested.

I decided against getting up to work with Bert's gang the next morning. I stocked up at the supermarket and paid a week in advance at the campsite. Unlike Ross, I had money saved. Something better would come up. Most campsite residents said there was heaps of work about. I went to town and splashed out on a pie and cappuccino, then spent the afternoon in the library. After that day of rest, Ross and I tried watermelon picking. Easy work, but you didn't make much in a day. You couldn't throw the melons faster than the person loading the tractor wanted to catch them. The ganger, a Turkish guy, invited us around to his caravan in the evening. He used some of our earnings to buy tons of KFC for dinner. We weren't impressed, not being huge fans of the colonel's greasy chicken. 'I warned you the Turks were dodgy!' a woman at the campsite reminded me when I told her about it. She had been there fifteen bloody years, working at the watermelon factory, where, from what I understood, all day long they washed melons with a chemical mixture.

We moved on to pumpkin picking with some Danish girls from the campsite who had a car. The Aussie pumpkin farmer didn't give a shit how hard we worked. He was thrilled to have those girls around, and of course, he only paid per pumpkin. After a hot day's work, we found an irrigation stream and jumped in. We drove back to the campsite, car stereo booming, the girls looking great in their wet clothes. But the joy came with pain because the situation only lasted a day. As we thought they might, the girls drove off somewhere less boring the next morning.

Only cotton chipping paid an hourly wage that'd allow us to save. I considered working for Bert again, but Ross

didn't have that option. I ran into the Harry Potter reader
again. I could hardly not, his van was next to my tent.
I seemed to meet a lot of people who slept in vans. 'I
wouldn't work for him either,' he said when I told him
what'd happened to Ross. 'He's a bastard that Bert.' My
neighbour knew how to deal with people like Bert: 'Fuck
them up with a baseball bat. The key thing is to get them
from behind in the back of the knee, so they go down fast.
I know these things, mate. I used to bash people for fifty
bucks.'

I had no clue if he was making this up. He didn't look like
much, just a small to medium-sized Aussie, blond and sun-
burnt. We kept talking and he shared his backstory with
me. At age nineteen, after repeated trouble with the cops
over fighting at rodeo meets and stealing cars, the courts
gave him the choice of jail or the army. Not surprisingly,
he chose the army but didn't like it much. Among other
things, they didn't give you enough toilet paper to wipe
your arse properly.

'Only three or four sheets.'

'Why was that?' I asked innocently.

'Why do you think? Because toilet paper is expensive?
No, shit for brains, to toughen you up! Ha ha.'

I'd exposed myself as a softy with such a stupid question.

He claimed that he ended up shooting his commanding
officer in the bum during a training exercise. He didn't
explain the exact fallout, but he seemed happy the way
things had turned out. Perhaps because my question about
toilet paper had made him laugh, he decided to help me
out: 'A couple of workers left the campsite today, mate. I

have some space in my gang now, come along tomorrow and see how you go.'

So, the next day I joined the team of Clive the Harry Potter reader. I got Ross along too. At first, Clive watched us like a hawk and threatened to fire us several times for missing weeds. The rest of his team consisted of three rodeo cowboys and two young Pommie couples who looked like they were going to collapse from sunstroke. 'It's unbelievable to me they can't take a couple of hours of heat,' Clive said. He warmed to Ross and me when we looked fresh at the end of our first day. There was some hope for us.

After several productive weeks, no more cotton fields in the area needed chipping. Clive got us a gig in another town doing the same thing with sunflowers. We camped out in a park. Some took their tents along. Others didn't bother, a sleeping bag was enough. On our first night, we tried the local pub for a laugh. It featured some ruinous-looking locals none too impressed by our presence. The park, with its long drop toilet and billabong you could swim in, was the better place to hang out and have a few beers. One evening, a girl showed up to see Clive and he took her into his van. She certainly wasn't a looker, Clive himself said so—but, he warned, 'Sometimes you've got to get one away.'

'He's a legend,' Ross said to me, out of earshot of the rest. 'Makes me miss that time with the Dutch girl in my van. You remember that, Ed?'

'Yes, but only because you mention it every couple of days.'

In the evenings, after a game of aquatic rugby in the billabong, we built a fire and Clive told us stories. Most had something to do with him breaking bones rodeo riding or patrolling the Northern Territory coastline when he was in the army. He suggested some jobs we could do up north once the chipping season ended, like rounding up and driving cattle if we could ride a motorbike. He remembered setting out once in the outback, taking cattle towards a gleaming water reservoir that appeared to be a few kilometres away. This was a trick of the mirage. It took all day to get to the reservoir. He was good at telling stories.

Another option was working on a cattle boat to Indonesia, getting paid to hose down the shit. Not quite a beach holiday in Bali, and something Clive hadn't lowered himself to do, but some of his rodeo mates had. I found myself considering this option. After my time on the Kurrus, I didn't see myself driving cattle on a motorbike, hosing non-smelly cow shit wouldn't be so bad. I imagined myself stepping off the boat in a sweltering hot port in Indonesia full of barnacled fishing boats.

Clive had never left Australia, and with so much more of it to see, he didn't see the point of going overseas. Unafraid of the world and free from job interviews, Clive didn't need to be fake. Sure, he got sick of chipping, but there was always the change of seasons and something different to do.

The sunflowers lasted ten days. On the drive back to the campsite, one British guy wanted Clive to stop so he could take a pee. Clive swore and shouted 'No!' several times, but finally in response to continuing requests said,

'Sure!' Clive stopped, let the guy out, and sped off while he was doing the business. The pisser hurriedly did up his fly and sprinted after us, only to get a face full of dust for his efforts. His girlfriend screamed at Clive, who told her she could get out too if she wanted. We were about fifteen kilometres from the campsite at that stage. She wisely refused his offer. That was Clive's kind of humour. Ross laughed his arse off too. Rather unsympathetic of him I felt considering what he'd gone through with Bert. The aggrieved party in this case was more forgiving and never plotted vengeance against Clive as far as I know.

'Done it yet?' I asked Ross for the fiftieth time. He'd showed up to check what I had on the campsite BBQ. He was terrible at buying his own food. This was our second day back from the sunflower mission, and we hadn't found a new gig yet.

'Yeah, I have. Finally got the bastard.'

'Geez, you found where Bert stays!'

'Yep, in a tent at a small campsite on the way to those cotton fields. He has the nicest set-up I've seen. He's got a quality air mattress. His tent is pitched right by the swimming pool.'

'Good for Bert. So, how does it feel?'

'OK, not bad.'

'You don't sound too happy about your latest achievement, though. Did something go wrong?'

'Nothing, next time I'll do the shit first and take it along in a bag, or take toilet paper, my arse was stuck to my undies all the way back.'

'I hope you've showered.'

'Yes, don't worry.'

'Did you walk all the way? How far?'

'Around ten kilometres.'

'What commitment.'

'It's not like there's a bus service.'

'Why didn't you wipe your arse at the campground toilet?'

'I didn't see one and I didn't want to hang around and ask.'

Surely some skid marks were a small price to pay for the sweet revenge of shitting in Bert's tent, but some of us want everything to go perfectly.

'Want a sausage and a piece of bread?'

'Yeah, cheers, mate.'

'Mission accomplished, then. You going to stay on here? Bert might put two and two together. Although, I'll bet you aren't his only enemy.'

'No, I'm off to Victoria, fancy it, mate?'

'No, I think I'll stick around. Clive's talking about a corn plantation that needs chipping. I'm going to save a few more bucks and head to Thailand for a holiday.'

'Good for you. Can I have another sausage?'

'Sure, here you go ... but slow down, you'll give yourself indigestion.'

After we'd finished eating, Ross took off to do his laundry leaving me to clean the grill.

***

Thank you for reading *Smoko,* please consider leaving a review on Amazon and/or Goodreads.